The Usborne of
soccer skills

THE
USBORNE BOOK
OF
SOCCER SKILLS

Gill Harvey, Jonathan Sheikh-Miller,
Richard Dungworth and Clive Gifford

Designed by Stephen Wright and Neil Francis

Illustrations by Bob Bond
Photographs by Chris Cole
Additional photographs by Shaun Botterill

Consultant: John Shiels
Photographic manipulation by John Russell
With thanks to Phil Darren, Peter Bonetti and Nasira Sheikh-Miller

CONTENTS

PITCH AND PLAYERS

If you are keen to become a good soccer player, the first
thing you need to do is become familiar with a number
of special soccer words. These two pages introduce some
basic terms that you'll come across as you read this book
and which you'll hear used when you play soccer.

FINDING YOUR WAY AROUND THE PITCH

If you kick the ball towards
your opponents' goal, you are
playing it **upfield**. Towards
your own goal is **downfield**.

The **wings** are the edges
of the pitch along either
touchline. A ball played
across from either wing
to the middle of the
pitch is a **cross**.

The third of
the pitch nearest
to your own goal
is your team's
defending third.

The middle
third of the
pitch is the
midfield.

The third of the
pitch nearest your
opponents' goal is
your team's
attacking third.

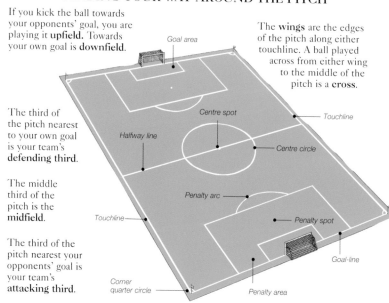

Goal area

Centre spot

Touchline

Halfway line

Centre circle

Penalty arc

Touchline

Penalty spot

Penalty area

Goal-line

Corner
quarter circle

THE REFEREE

The **referee** is an
official who controls
a soccer match. It is
his job to decide
when to stop and
restart play. He
uses a whistle and
special arm signals
(which you'll read
about later on) to
show the players
his decisions.

REFEREE'S ASSISTANTS

Two **referee's
assistants** help
the referee by
watching the game
from opposite sides
of the pitch. Each
assistant uses a flag
to signal to the
referee if the ball
goes off of the pitch
or if he sees a player
breaking the rules.

TYPES OF PLAYER

A soccer team is made up of a **goalkeeper**, who guards his team's goal, and ten **outfield** players. Each outfield player **marks** a particular member of the other team. This means keeping close to him to stop him from receiving or moving with the ball.

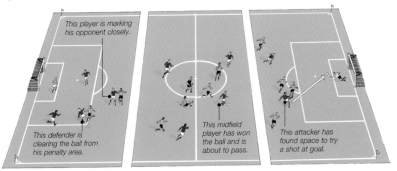

This player is marking his opponent closely.

This defender is clearing the ball from his penalty area.

This midfield player has won the ball and is about to pass.

This attacker has found space to try a shot at goal.

Defenders play mostly in their defending third. Their main job is to prevent the other team's players from having a chance to score.

Midfield players are the link between defence and attack. They move the ball upfield, and try to pass to a team-mate who can score.

Attackers push upfield into the attacking third, hoping to receive a pass which will give them a chance to shoot at goal.

WHAT DOES OFFSIDE MEAN?

You are not allowed to play the ball if you are in an **offside** position (see page 78). You are offside if you are nearer to your opponents' goal-line than the ball at the moment it is passed to you, unless there are two or more opposition players at least as close to their goal-line. You can't be offside if you are within your own half of the pitch.

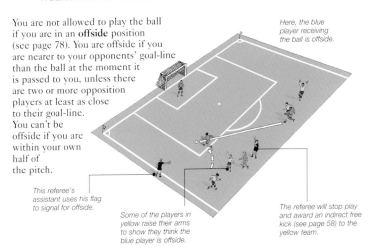

Here, the blue player receiving the ball is offside.

This referee's assistant uses his flag to signal for offside.

Some of the players in yellow raise their arms to show they think the blue player is offside.

The referee will stop play and award an indirect free kick (see page 58) to the yellow team.

GETTING STARTED

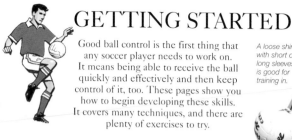

Good ball control is the first thing that any soccer player needs to work on. It means being able to receive the ball quickly and effectively and then keep control of it, too. These pages show you how to begin developing these skills. It covers many techniques, and there are plenty of exercises to try.

A loose shirt with short or long sleeves is good for training in.

WHAT DO I NEED?

Don't wear shorts or tracksuit bottoms that are tight. They will slow you down.

All you need to train with are a soccer ball and some markers. Special sports markers are shown here, but you can use bags or sweaters. Wear loose, comfortable clothing such as a tracksuit or shorts and T-shirt. On most surfaces trainers are fine, but soccer boots are best if you are playing on muddy ground.

Shinpads protect you against hard tackles.

Sports marker

WARMING UP

To have good ball control, you need to be able to move your whole body well. Being able to twist, turn and keep your balance are key skills for many control techniques.

Do this exercise in pairs. More than one pair can play at once. It is a good warm-up exercise which will improve your balance and movement.

6m (20ft)

Mark out a 6m (20ft) square. Scatter six or seven markers inside it. Decide who will be attacker and who will defend.

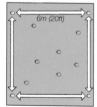

The attacker dribbles forward, weaving around the markers. The defender tries to stop him reaching the other side.

You cannot touch each other or leave the square. If the defender forces the attacker off the square, he has won.

GETTING THE FEEL OF THE BALL

If you are used to playing around with a soccer ball you will probably already have some idea of how the ball responds when you touch it in different ways. This is what it means to have a feel for the ball. This page looks more closely at how this works and how you can use the different parts of your foot to do different things.

The inside of your foot is used most often. Use it for controlling, dribbling and passing.

The outside of your foot is useful for turning, dribbling and passing the ball to the side.

Your instep is the most powerful part of your foot. It is best for kicking, especially shooting.

Your heel is not often used, but it is good for flicking the ball backwards or a quick reverse pass.

It is very difficult to control the ball with the tips of your toes. You should hardly ever use them.

It is risky to use the sole of your foot to control the ball, but you use it for some trick moves.

This exercise helps you to get a feel for the parts of your foot that you use most often – the inside, outside and instep (see left).

Lay out seven markers 2m (6ft) apart in a zig-zag line. Push the ball from the first to the second with the outside of your foot.

The outside of the foot tends to tap the ball away from you. To keep it in control you need a gentle touch.

At the second marker, start using the inside of your foot.

This is the easiest way to push the ball, as it naturally rolls in front of you.

At the next marker, use your instep. Tap the ball into the air, let it bounce once, then tap it up again.

This is basic 'juggling', which you can do without letting the ball bounce. Find out more about juggling on page 10.

At the following marker, start the sequence again. Try to get used to using both your left and your right foot.

HOW TO MEASURE

All the measurements for the exercises and games in this book are given in metres (m) and feet (ft). It's a good idea to think of 1m (3ft) as roughly being about one big stride. You can then measure out the correct distances easily in strides. So, don't worry about having to get the measurements exactly right.

BALL CONTROL

Being in control means knowing how to receive the ball
from any angle, and then being able to run with it
and pass confidently. Here you'll learn the
basics and a few tricks.

MOVING ON

Once you have a basic feel for the ball you are on the way to developing good control. The next stage is to do plenty of practice to develop your skills. Things like juggling the ball are good for this, but you also need to work on special control methods. Here you can find out about the basic techniques that will help you.

JUGGLING

Although you rarely use juggling in an actual game, it helps you to develop the quick reactions, tight ball control and concentration that you need in order to play well.

To get the ball into the air, roll your foot back over the top of the ball, then hook it under and flick the ball up.

Keep the ball in the air by bouncing it off your foot. Hold your foot out flat. If you point your toes up, you will probably lose control.

As you develop your control, pass from one foot to the other, or bounce it up further into the air so that you juggle it on your knee.

Keep your eye on the ball all the time.

You could try juggling the ball on your shoulder and with your head.

JUGGLING GAME

Work on your juggling with a group of friends. Choose someone to be a caller. All of you dribble until the caller shouts 'Up!'

Everyone flicks the ball up and juggles. The last one to keep the ball in the air wins. When he drops it, you all start dribbling again.

RECEIVING THE BALL

FIRST TOUCH

Controlling the ball as you receive it is one of the most important skills you can learn. Everything else you do depends on this, so it's well worth spending plenty of time on it. These are the main points to remember.

1. To get your timing right, you need to judge the flight of the ball carefully.

2. Don't just hope the ball will come straight to you. Move into line with it.

This player is demonstrating good first touch. The ball is moving and in a good position to be played away.

3. Decide early which part of your body you will use to control the ball.

4. Once you have the ball, don't hesitate. Decide on your next move quickly.

The moment you make contact with the ball is called the 'first touch.' A good first touch keeps the ball moving and places it a short distance from your feet. To develop this skill, you need to 'cushion' the ball.

WHAT IS CUSHIONING?

Cushioning means taking the speed out of the ball, just as a cushion would if it was attached to your body. It slows the ball down without making it bounce away. Here you can see how cushioning works in practice.

As the ball travels towards you, position your foot in line with it to receive it.

On making contact, relax your foot and let it travel back with the ball.

The speed of the ball is absorbed. It slows down and you can play it away.

11

FOOT CONTROL

Your feet are the parts of your body that you use most often to receive the ball. Remember that a good first touch keeps the ball moving, so use the inside, outside or instep of your foot rather than your sole. Try to slow the ball down and position it in one smooth movement.

USING THE INSIDE OF YOUR FOOT

If you use the inside of your foot, you will be in a good position to play the ball away when you have cushioned it.

This player is balanced and in line with the ball.

Make sure you work on receiving with your left and your right foot.

Watch the ball as it approaches and place your foot in line with it. Balance on one leg with your receiving foot turned out.

As you receive the ball with the inside of your foot, relax your leg and foot so that they travel back with it.

The ball should drop just in front of your feet. Look around you and play it away to the left or right as quickly as possible.

USING THE OUTSIDE OF YOUR FOOT

If you are going to use the outside of your foot, decide to do so quickly and turn so that your side faces the ball.

Lift your leg to receive the ball with the outside of your foot. Relax your foot back and down to the ground.

Push the ball to the outside with the same foot, as you can see here, or across your body with either foot.

USING YOUR INSTEP

To control the ball with your instep, make sure you are facing the ball with your arms out for balance.

Lift your foot, but keep it flat. If you point your toes up the ball will probably bounce off them.

Just as you receive the ball, lower your foot to the ground, letting the ball drop off it in front of you.

THINGS TO AVOID

Try not to stop the ball dead. If you do, you have to touch it again before you can play your next move.

If the ball bounces off your foot and ends up a long way from you, you waste time chasing it.

PASS AND CONTROL EXERCISE

Do this exercise with a friend. Make a 'gate' with two markers and stand with the gate between you. Pass the ball through the gate so that your partner has to control it.

He turns and passes the ball down the outside of the gate. Control it, turn and pass it back through the gate or down the other side of it. Carry on passing and receiving like this.

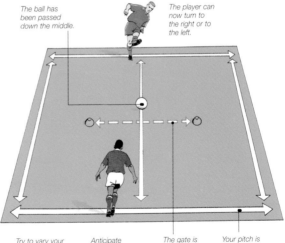

The ball has been passed down the middle.

The player can now turn to the right or to the left.

Try to vary your passes as much as possible, but keep them low.

Anticipate which way the ball will come and run for it.

The gate is about 2m (6ft) wide.

Your pitch is about 5m (16ft) wide.

HIGHER BALLS

When a ball comes at you from a higher angle, there are several things you can do. Depending on where you position yourself and how high the ball is, you can receive it with your foot, thigh or chest. Whichever you decide upon, you still use a cushioning technique to take the pace out of the ball.

USING YOUR THIGH

If you cushion the ball properly it shouldn't sting your leg.

Watch the ball carefully so that you can judge where it will land.

Bend your knee to meet the ball, using your arms for balance. On making contact, straighten your leg gradually so that the ball drops off your thigh in front of your feet.

USING YOUR FOOT

Keeping your arms out for balance, lift your leg to meet the ball. Catch it with the inside of your foot.

Without hooking your foot completely under the ball, drop it down to the ground, dragging the ball down with it.

USING YOUR CHEST

Your chest is good for cushioning because it is bigger than any other part of your body. Keep your hands open, because clenching your fist makes your chest muscles tighten and they need to relax. Keep your arms out of the way, too, to avoid handling the ball.

Put your arms back and open up your chest as the ball approaches you.

As the ball makes contact with you, cushion it by letting yourself relax.

Bring your shoulders in and hollow your chest, so that the ball rolls off you.

The ball drops to the ground gently and you are able to play your next move.

HIGH BALL PRACTICE

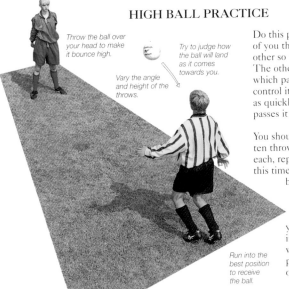

Throw the ball over your head to make it bounce high.

Try to judge how the ball will land as it comes towards you.

Vary the angle and height of the throws.

Run into the best position to receive the ball.

Do this practice in pairs. One of you throws the ball to the other so that it bounces once. The other person decides which part of the body to control it with, controls it as quickly as possible and passes it back.

You should swap over after ten throws. After ten throws each, repeat the exercise, but this time without letting the ball bounce.

If you do this practice regularly your ball control will improve a lot and you will be able to receive passes from all kinds of angles.

INSIDE FOOT KICKS

Now that you have developed some basic ball control, you can move on to learning how to kick the ball accurately, or pass, to another player as well as shoot at goal. Here, you focus on the inside of your foot, which is the area you use most for kicking.

THE PUSH PASS

This is a low kick for short distances. It is called a pass, but you can use it to shoot at close range. It is easy to learn, and accurate.

1. Swing your foot back, turning it out so that it is almost at right angles to your other foot.

2. Keep your ankle firm and make contact with the middle of the ball (see page 17).

3. Follow through in a smooth, level movement, keeping your eye on the ball the whole time. Keep your foot low – try not to sweep it upwards, as this will make the ball rise.

ACCURACY PRACTICE

Work with a friend. Place two markers 60cm (2ft) apart. One of you stands 1m (3ft) in front of them, the other 1m (3ft) behind. Try to pass to each other through the gap. Score a point for each success.

After five passes each, move another 1m (3ft) apart and start again. Carry on until you are 10m (33ft) apart. The player with the most points wins.

2m (6ft)

The kicker is keeping his foot low and his eye on the ball.

This practice may seem easy to start with, but as you both move apart, it will become a lot harder to make accurate passes.

THE INSIDE FOOT SWERVE

Swerving the ball is really useful when passing or shooting. You have more control with the inside of your foot than the outside, so it is best to learn the inside foot swerve first.

Direction of ball
Kicking foot
Non-kicking foot

The ball should swerve out, then swing back in again.

Follow through freely, your foot rising to follow the direction of the ball.

1. Keep your eyes on the ball as you swing your leg back. Your non-kicking foot should be well out of the way of the ball.

2. Use the side of your foot to kick. The secret is to kick the ball in the right place. (See above).

WHERE TO KICK THE BALL

You make the ball go in different directions by knowing which part of it to kick. To work out which part is which, think of it as having two sides, a top and a bottom. The diagrams below show you how this will be illustrated.

When you are told to kick one side of the ball, you see a diagram of it as it looks from above when you kick. Kick to the left or right.

Diagrams like this show the top or bottom of the ball by looking at it side on, so imagine what it would look like from the side as you kick.

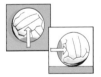

When you are told to kick the ball through the middle, this means both the middle from above and the middle from the side.

From above, you see the right side.

From the side, you see the middle.

If you are told just one part of the ball to kick, for example the right side, you can assume you kick through the middle from the other angle.

OUTSIDE FOOT KICKS

When you use the outside of your foot to kick the ball, you can disguise your movements very well. Also, because the ball is to one side of you, you are able to move freely and pass or shoot as you run. However, accuracy and control can be difficult, so you will need to practise hard.

FLICKING THE BALL TO THE SIDE

This move is particularly useful when you are under pressure and you receive a fast pass from the side which you do not have time to control. The trick is to let the ball bounce off the outside of your foot, while at the same time directing it to a team-mate with a flick of your ankle.

Make contact with little toe area

You don't need any backswing.

1. Keep your back to anyone marking you. Turn the outside of your foot towards the ball.

2. Don't cushion the ball as it makes contact. Direct it out to the side with a flick of your foot.

3. If the ball has been kicked through the middle, it should stay low but fast. Try to direct it into the path of another player.

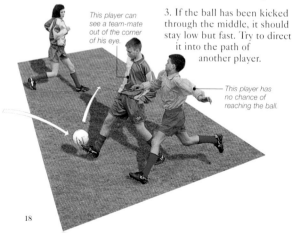

This player can see a team-mate out of the corner of his eye.

This player has no chance of reaching the ball.

FLICK GAME

A   B

10m (33ft)

This is for two players (A and B). Mark out a 10m (33ft) square. Start in the two top corners.

A

B

B runs across the square as A passes the ball into his path. B returns it with a flick pass.

A

B

A pushes the ball to B, then starts to run. B feeds the ball for him to flick back. Carry on like this.

OUTSIDE FOOT SWERVES

This kick makes the ball swerve away to the side. It is a difficult kick to master, and you need to be quite strong to make it go a long way. However, you don't need to control the ball before you kick it and you can do it as you run, so it is an ideal kick to use for shots at goal.

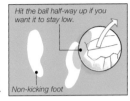

Hit the ball half-way up if you want it to stay low.

Non-kicking foot

LOFTED SWERVES

A 'lofted' kick means a high kick. If you want an outside foot swerve to go higher and clear other players, kick the ball through its lower half and not through the middle.

Kicking foot swings under the ball

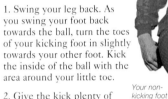

1. Swing your leg back. As you swing your foot back towards the ball, turn the toes of your kicking foot in slightly towards your other foot. Kick the inside of the ball with the area around your little toe.

2. Give the kick plenty of follow-through, sweeping your leg across your body. The ball should swerve out away from you.

Your non-kicking foot should be well out of the way of your kicking foot.

PAIRS PRACTICE

Pass the ball down a straight line. Try to make it swing out from the line and back in again by using outside foot swerves.

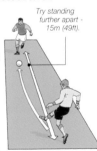

Try standing further apart - 15m (49ft).

USING YOUR INSTEP

Your instep is the area over your laces. It is the most powerful part of your foot, so use it if you want to kick the ball a long way or kick it very hard. At first you may accidentally use your toes, but this will improve with practice.

THE LOW INSTEP DRIVE

You can use this kick as you are running to send the ball a long way. It is quite difficult to make it accurate, but the secret of success is to hit the ball right through the middle.

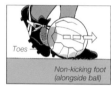

Toes

Non-kicking foot (alongside ball)

Place your non-kicking foot close to the ball.

1. Swing your kicking leg well back, so that your heel almost reaches up to your behind.

2. Point your toes toward the ground and make contact with the middle of the ball.

3. Swing your foot onwards in the direction of the ball, but make sure your ankle is still stretched out towards the ground as you follow through. This is the key to keeping the kick low.

INSTEP PASS GAME

Use this game to help you develop your basic instep kicking technique. It is best with four people, but you could play with any number above two – change the shape of the pitch to make a corner for each player.

Mark out a 30m (98ft) square. Label yourselves A, B, C and D and stand at its four corners.

A passes to B at an angle so that he has to run on to it. B receives it and passes it at an angle to C.

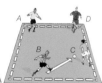

After passing, B stays where he is. C runs on to the ball and passes to D, and so on around the square.

THE LOFTED DRIVE

The lofted drive is a long, high kick. The technique for doing it is similar to the technique for low instep kicks, but you kick the ball in a different place and let your foot swing right up when you follow through.

Kicking the ball on its lower half makes it rise.

1. Approach the ball from a slight angle. Swing your leg back, looking down at the ball as you do so.

2. Make contact with the lower half of the ball, so that your instep reaches slightly under it.

3. Follow through with a sweeping movement, letting your leg swing up across your body.

GAINING POWER AND HEIGHT

You will find that your drives will be higher and more powerful if you lean back as you swing your leg towards the ball. This usually happens naturally, though you may find it easier if you kick from slightly further away.

This player leans well back, showing his confidence in kicking the ball powerfully.

PERFECTING YOUR TECHNIQUE

To improve your lofted drives you may think you just need to kick the ball harder, but it is more important to develop your technique. In this game you practise drives that need to be accurate as well as powerful to reach their target.

Four of you (A, B, C, D) can work at this by marking out a row of four boxes, all 10m (33ft) square. Each of you stands in a box, which you cannot move out of.

A and B try to lob the ball over C and D. Score a point for each success. If C or D manages to intercept the ball, he takes the place of the player who kicked it.

D intercepts the ball and takes the place of A.

21

VOLLEYING

Volleying means kicking the ball before it has hit the ground. It is a fast and exciting way to play the ball, because you don't spend time controlling it before playing it. This gives the ball pace and makes it harder for your opponents to guess where it is going to go.

FRONT VOLLEY

Front volleys are probably the easiest volleys to do, but you still need quick reactions to do them well. You use your instep to receive the ball, so you need to be facing it. If you are not, it can be difficult to keep your balance and the volley may go out of control.

Kick through the lower half of the ball.

The ball makes contact with your instep.

1. Lift your knee as the ball approaches. Point your toes and stretch out your ankle.

If you make contact later, your non-kicking foot should be closer to the ball.

2. As you direct the ball away, try to keep your head forward over your knee.

LEARNING TO VOLLEY

Work with a friend. Stand 3m (10ft) apart. Drop the ball onto your foot and volley it to him gently for him to catch.

3m (10ft)

VARYING THE HEIGHT

If you want to send the ball high, perhaps to clear a defender, get your foot right under the ball.

To stop the ball rising too much, lift your foot up over the ball slightly after making contact.

SIDE VOLLEY

Side volleys are more difficult than front volleys. You need quick reactions, as you do for any volley, but the leg movement that you have to do is also quite tricky – you need to be able to balance on one leg while you are leaning sideways.

1. Watch the ball as it comes towards you so that you can judge the right angle to meet it.

2. As you lift your outside leg up, make sure that the shoulder nearest the ball isn't in the way.

3. Swing your leg up and round in a sideways movement so that your instep makes contact.

4. Follow through in the direction of the ball by swinging your leg right across your body.

HIGHER AND LOWER

If you want to keep the ball low, try to make contact with the ball just above the middle.

To make the ball rise over the heads of other players, kick it just below the middle.

SIDE ACTION PRACTICE

Because the leg movement is the most difficult part of this volley, you may find it helps to practise over an obstacle. Make or find something that is almost as high as your hip, and try swinging your leg over it. You can put the ball on top of it if you want. If it is too high to reach, begin with a lower obstacle.

TRIO VOLLEY GAME

When you can do the leg movement, play this with two friends. A throws the ball to B, who volleys to C. C throws the ball for A to volley, and so on.

Score a point each time you volley accurately. The player with the most points after ten volleys each is the winner.

MORE ABOUT VOLLEYING

Much of the skill in volleying depends on having the
confidence to strike the ball early. If you take the initiative and
go for the ball instead of waiting for it to reach you, you will
find it easier to control its direction. All the volleys on these
pages are most effective if you act quickly and decisively.

THE HALF-VOLLEY

To do a half-volley, you
kick the ball just as it
bounces. If you kick it
correctly, it should stay low
and also be quite powerful.
Point your toes, stretch out
your ankle, then kick the
ball with your instep. Your
knee should make a firm
snapping action.

*Once it is
kicked, the
ball shoots
off very fast.*

*Your non-kicking foot is alongside
the ball and a little behind it.*

1. Judge the flight of the ball
and position yourself just
behind where it will land.
Take a short backswing.

2. Keeping your head
forward so that it is in line
with your knee, kick the ball
as soon as it hits the ground.

VOLLEYS IN THE AIR

If the ball is very
high, you may need
to jump for it and
volley it in the air.

Use a front or side
volley technique,
depending on the
angle of the ball.

Your timing has to
be especially good,
so keep your eye on
the ball all the time.

Watch the flight of
the ball as you land.
Get ready to follow
the ball forward.

THE 'LAY-OFF' VOLLEY

'Laying the ball off' means playing the ball to another player when you don't have much time to play it yourself. To play a 'lay-off' volley, take the ball early and direct it out to the left or right with your first touch.

Instead of using your instep, turn your foot to use the inside or outside of it.

Make contact with the middle of the ball, or slightly above the middle to send the ball down.

Here, a defender is in a position to challenge the player receiving the ball. He can see that a team-mate is in a better position to play the ball forward, so he lays it off to him.

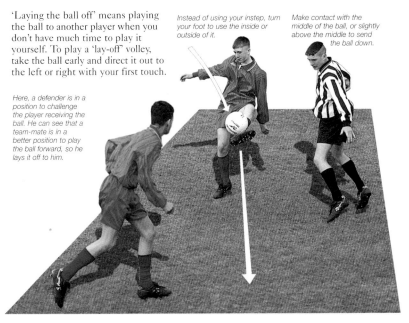

ONE BOUNCE GAME

In this game, you can make use of all the volleys you have learned. It is for three or more players, though it is best with about six. Each player begins with five lives.

Stand in a circle 10m (33ft) across. One player kicks the ball high to another player, who lets it bounce once then volleys it to someone else. Use any type of volley.

You lose a life for missing or mis-hitting a volley. The winner is the last with any lives left. Next, play without letting the ball bounce (apart from half-volleys).

STAR VOLLEY

Here, Dimitar Berbatov of Bulgaria strikes a side volley at goal while playing against Croatia. He has his eye on the ball as he kicks.

CHIPPING

The chip is a kick which makes the ball rise very quickly into the air. It is not very powerful, but it is ideal for lifting the ball over opponents' heads, especially the goalkeeper's.

Here, the player watches the ball as it rises up away from him.

BASIC TECHNIQUE

The secret of the chip is to stab at the ball without following through. The area just below your instep acts like a wedge which punches the ball into the air.

Direction of ball

1. Face the ball straight on. It is almost impossible to chip from the side. Take a short backswing.

2. Bring your foot down with a sharp stabbing action, aiming your foot at the bottom of the ball.

3. Your foot kicks into the ground as it hits the ball, which is why there is no follow-through. This should happen naturally – it doesn't really matter if your leg does swing up as long as the ball flies into the air.

TECHNIQUE TIPS

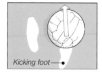

Kicking foot

Your non-kicking foot should be alongside the ball and close to it, only about 20cm (8in) away.

Vary your chips by leaning forward or back. If you lean back, the chip will not fly as high, but it may go further.

CHIPPING PRACTICE

You can chip the ball when it is still or when it is moving. It is probably easiest to do if you run on to the ball as it is moving towards you. This exercise allows you to practise your basic technique with the ball coming towards you.

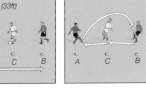

The exercise is for three players. Lay out three markers 10m (33ft) apart.

C passes along the ground to A. A chips it over C to B, who plays it back to C.

C plays the ball along the ground to B, who chips it to A. A passes it to C.

If A or B mis-hits a chip, he goes into the middle and C takes his place.

COMPARING HIGH KICKS

It is difficult to chip very far, so use a lofted drive for longer kicks. Here, you practise both types of kick. You need two or more players. Divide into two groups. Put six markers in a row, 5m (16ft) apart, and mark out a 5m (16ft) area around each one.

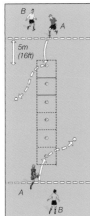
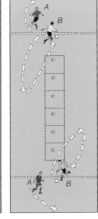
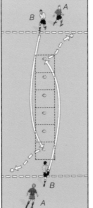

Stand 5m (16ft) from each end of the row. The first player tries to chip into the first area, aiming for the marker in the middle.

Score 10 for hitting the area, 20 for the marker. The next player gets the ball while you go to the back of the queue.

All of you try hitting the first area, then move on to the next. Use lofted drives for the last three areas, instead of chips.

To save running to collect the ball, pick up the opposite group's long drives. Keep playing, making a note of the score.

TRICK MOVES

Sometimes a trick move is just what you need to take your opponents by surprise. Some of them can be quite risky, though, so only use them in the attacking third of the field where losing the ball does not put your team in too much danger. Some of these tricks are easy to perform and others need quite a lot of practice.

THE BACKHEEL PASS

To do a backheel pass, you kick the ball back with your heel, or sometimes your sole. You can completely surprise your opponents if you do it quickly, and if there is a team-mate behind you to receive it.

For a basic backheel pass, keep your foot level as you kick so that it doesn't jab down at the ball.

To get a different angle or to disguise your movements, you can cross one leg over the other.

You can roll the ball back with your sole. Point your toes down and kick the middle of the ball.

THE CHEST PASS

Sometimes, when the ball comes at you from a high angle, you have very little time to control it before passing it. You can use your chest to redirect it, but only if the ball is travelling fast – your chest will tend to cushion a slow ball.

Tense your chest muscles and stick your chest out to make a hard surface for the ball to bounce off. Redirect it to a team-mate by turning quickly to the left or right as it reaches you.

This player cannot step back to receive the ball at a lower angle.

This team-mate is not as closely marked, so he is in a good position to receive the ball and play it away.

THE OVERHEAD KICK

This is a spectacular and exciting kick, but it is also very risky. Never try it in the defending third of the field, or in a crowded area where you might kick someone. Also, remember that if you fall you cannot follow up your pass, so make sure other players can follow it up instead.

1. The ball should be at about head height. Take off on one leg, jumping backwards.

2. Keep your eye on the ball and swing your kicking foot up over head height.

At the highest point of the kick, your foot is at other players' head height. This means you need to be especially careful not to kick someone.

3. At the highest point of your jump, strike the ball with your instep.

Try to kick the ball through the middle.

4. Cushion your fall by relaxing and rolling on your shoulder. This will stop you from hurting your wrists.

VARIATIONS

If the ball is not quite as high, you can do overhead kicks while keeping your non-kicking foot on the ground. Lift your kicking foot up to reach the ball, keeping your arms out for balance.

If the ball is further away from you, try the 'scissors' kick. It is a bit like the side volley (see page 23), but you jump and kick while you are sideways on in the air.

HOW TO PRACTISE

Practise on soft grass or a cushioned mat. Get a friend to help you and stand about 5m (16ft) apart. Your friend throws the ball to you for you to kick.

At first, work on landing safely. Once you are sure about this, work on timing your jump, because timing is the main secret of success.

TURNING

Once you have received the ball and controlled it, you need to move off with it as fast as possible before an opponent can challenge you. You improve your chances of doing this effectively if you can turn quickly and sharply, so it is worth learning several turns to outwit your opponents.

Marker

TURNING 'OFF-LINE'

When you receive the ball, always try to turn immediately and take it off in another direction. This is what is meant by taking the ball 'off-line'. If you keep running in the same direction, it is too easy for your opponents to guess where the ball will go next. They will quickly be able to reach you and tackle you.

The ball has been passed to a player who is being closely marked.

This line shows the 'on-line' route that the player must try to avoid taking.

Instead of taking the on-line route, the player reaches the ball and turns off-line.

DOING AN INSIDE HOOK

As you receive the ball, watch out for approaching opponents and lean in the direction you want to go.

Drop your shoulder so that you are partly turned. Hook the inside of your foot around the ball.

Move off at a sharp angle, dragging the ball around with the inside of your foot. Accelerate away.

30

DOING AN OUTSIDE HOOK

To begin the turn, reach across your body and hook the ball at the bottom with the outside of your foot.

Sweep the ball around to the side with the same foot. Lean in the direction you want to go.

Turn to follow the path of the ball and accelerate away from your opponent as quickly as possible.

CONTROL AND TURNING EXERCISE

This exercise helps you to develop the different skills of controlling the ball and turning with it into one smooth movement. You will need three or more people.

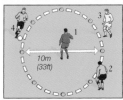 

1. Mark out a circle 10m (33ft) wide. Number the players. The highest (Player 4 here) has the ball and the lowest stands in the middle.

2. Player 4 begins the game by passing the ball into the middle. Player 1 controls it and turns with it. He can turn in any direction.

3. Player 1 dribbles the ball to the edge of the circle and Player 2 runs to the middle. Player 1 turns and passes the ball back to Player 2.

4. Player 2 controls the ball, turns and runs to the edge. Player 3 takes his place in the middle. After Player 3, Player 4 runs in, and so on.

STAR TURN

Portuguese attacker Cristiano Ronaldo is famous for his excellent ball control skills and speed.

Here, he very cleverly uses an outside hook to good effect, as he easily manages to pull the ball away from his Russian opponent.

If the defender mistimes his challenge from behind, he could give away a free kick in a dangerous position (see page 60).

DRIBBLING

Once you have possession of the ball, you may want to pass or shoot, but one of the most exciting parts of playing soccer is keeping the ball under your control and dribbling it up the field. If you watch a good dribbler, the ball seems almost stuck to his feet as he runs. This is what you should aim for.

BASIC TECHNIQUE

You can use your instep to dribble, especially for the first few touches. Be careful not to kick the ball very far.

You are free to run faster if you use the outside of your foot, but try not to tap the ball too far out to the side.

The inside of your foot may feel the most comfortable to use.

Be careful not to let the ball get under your feet.

MOVEMENT AND BALANCE

You need to be flexible and balanced to dribble well. To develop these skills, dribble around a slalom. Lay ten markers about 4m (13ft) apart in a zigzag line. Start to dribble down the line, weaving around the markers.

Try dribbling with different parts of your feet to see which feels most comfortable.

Keep the ball close to your feet. Try to exaggerate the twists and turns, leaning as far as you can as you run.

Keep as close to the path of the slalom as possible. Turn sharply at the markers.

In a game, you would need to look out for other players, so try to look around as you dribble.

Gradually increase your speed. If you find that you cannot lean as far, slow down again until you improve.

Try to run lightly on your toes, so that you can change direction quickly and easily.

TAG DRIBBLE

This game is for up to four people, though more people can play if you make the square bigger.

1. Lay out a 6 x 6m (20 x 20ft) square with four markers. Each player has a ball and stands in the square.

2. Dribble around the square. Try to 'tag' other players without being tagged yourself and without losing control of the ball.

3. Keep a score. You gain a point each time you tag someone, and if you are tagged, you lose a point.

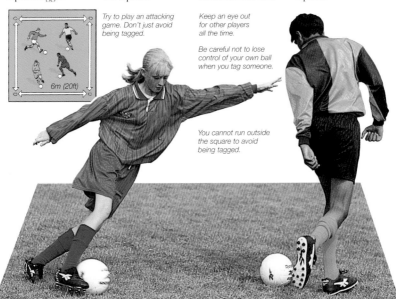

Try to play an attacking game. Don't just avoid being tagged.

Keep an eye out for other players all the time.

Be careful not to lose control of your own ball when you tag someone.

You cannot run outside the square to avoid being tagged.

6m (20ft)

IDEAL TECHNIQUE

Good dribbling should combine tight control with freedom of movement. Some people think that you should dribble with the outside of your foot as much as possible, because it gives you freedom to run and makes it easy for you to turn to the outside. You should have good control of the ball at all times.

Here, American DaMarcus Beasley uses his good dribbling skills to launch an attack on the opposition goal.

FEINTING

Feinting means fooling your opponents while you are
dribbling. It is also called 'selling a dummy'. Two things
will make your opponent move in a particular direction,
either the movement of your body or the movement of
the ball. Feinting uses the movement of your body.

A SIMPLE DUMMY

The simplest dummy or feint is
pretending to go one way, then
swerving and going
the other. Here,
Player 1
dribbles up
the field as
Player 2
comes to
challenge him.

Player 1

Player 2

Player 1 drops his
right shoulder,
making Player 2
think that he is
going to turn to
the right.

Player 2 moves to the
right, but Player 1
now swerves back to
the left. He dodges
around Player 2 and
accelerates
past him.

KEY FACTORS

Exaggerate
your dropped
shoulder and
body swerve
to fool your
opponent.

Accelerate
past your
opponent
before he
has time
to recover.

Be confident
when you
try to sell
a dummy,
or you
risk losing
the ball.

A STAR FEINT

Here, Brazilian superstar
Ronaldinho is about to
smoothly dummy past a
French opponent.

BASIC FEINTING PRACTICE

Work with a partner. Try to dribble past him, using a feint – you are not allowed just to push the ball past him and run.

If you get past him, turn and try again. If you don't, he dribbles past you instead. Score a point each time you get past.

GUESS AND DODGE GAME

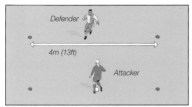

Defender

4m (13ft)

Attacker

The attacker here dodges to the left.

This makes the defender also turn to the left.

1. This is a game for two people with one ball. Both of you stand between two markers placed about 4m (13ft) apart.

2. Decide who will attack and who will defend. The attacker has the ball. The aim is for the attacker to reach a marker.

3. If the defender has his foot on one marker, the attacker has to go the other way. He cannot touch the matching marker.

4. Keep on playing until the attacker reaches a marker, then swap over so that you both have a turn at being attacker.

A good defender tries to watch the ball, not your movements. This game helps you to develop the speed and anticipation you need to beat him.

You need to be able to switch your balance from one foot to the other.

Once you see that your opponent is off balance, run for your marker quickly.

Here, the attacker has quickly turned to the right to reach the other marker.

ATTACKING

If you want to win a match, you have to have a
strong attack. This section teaches you some
great running, passing and crossing tactics,
and shows you how to turn a dead ball situation
into a deadly goal-scoring opportunity.

ATTACKING MOVES

Now that you have developed some ball control and
passing skills, the next stage is to work on some
attacking moves, or plays, with your team-mates. A
few simple passes can help your team move the ball
upfield past your opponents.

MAKING A BLINDSIDE RUN

One good way of finding space upfield is to make a run
behind an opponent's back, outside his field of view.
This is known as making a blindside run.

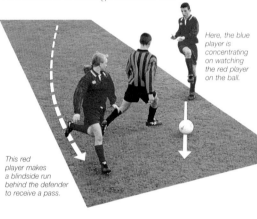

*Here, the blue
player is
concentrating
on watching
the red player
on the ball.*

*This red
player makes
a blindside run
behind the defender
to receive a pass.*

Above, a blindside run
forms the second part of a
'pass and run' attacking
move. Player A passes
to player B. As the
yellow player moves
in to challenge B, A makes
a run around his blindside.
Player B hits a return pass
upfield into A's path.

BEATING BALL-WATCHERS

Try to catch defenders 'ball-watching'.
This means paying too much attention to
play elsewhere on the pitch, instead of to
their own positions. Grab your chance to
make a blindside run into a good position.

*Here, the green player takes advantage of his marker's
lapse of concentration, making a blindside run behind him.*

OVERLAPPING

Doing an 'overlap run'
means running past a
team-mate on the ball
and into space
upfield, so that he
can pass the ball
back up to you. A
simple overlap
move, like the
one shown here,
is a particularly
good way of
pushing the
attack upfield
along one of
the wings.

*Here, player A passes to his
team-mate and follows his pass,
overlapping to receive a return ball.*

WALL PASSES

A wall pass, or 'one-two', is a great way of getting past a player. To do this, dribble straight at your opponent. Just before he challenges you, send a sideways pass to a team-mate. Your opponent will turn to follow the play, giving you a chance to sprint past him. Your team-mate acts as the wall, knocking the ball back into your path.

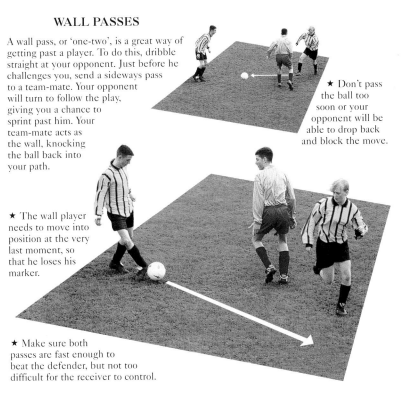

★ Don't pass the ball too soon or your opponent will be able to drop back and block the move.

★ The wall player needs to move into position at the very last moment, so that he loses his marker.

★ Make sure both passes are fast enough to beat the defender, but not too difficult for the receiver to control.

WALL PASS GAME

Mark out an area 24 x 6m (80 x 20ft) and divide it into four equal 'zones'. Five attackers and four defenders take up starting positions as shown.

The player with the ball tries to take it from one end to the other. He can dribble past a defender, or use a wall pass. He scores a point for each zone he crosses.

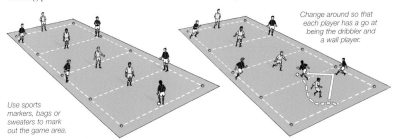

Change around so that each player has a go at being the dribbler and a wall player.

Use sports markers, bags or sweaters to mark out the game area.

BUILDING AN ATTACK

Good attacking play needs team co-ordination and co-operation, as well as individual running and passing skills. To build an attack, you and your team-mates need to work together to make the most of the space available on the pitch, and to keep the defence guessing.

GIVING AN ATTACK WIDTH

If all your attacking players gather around the player on the ball, so that they are clustered together in one area of the pitch, your attack will be easy to defend against.

Spread out across the pitch, so that your opponents are forced to defend across its whole width. By passing across the pitch, you can quickly change the path of attack.

WING ATTACKS

Your opponents will try to protect the central area of their defensive third, in front of their goal. You can often push upfield into attack more easily by passing the ball to a team-mate on the wing, where there is more space.

Here, English defender Ashley Cole beats his opponent on the wing.

GIVING AN ATTACK DEPTH

If your players form a flat line across the pitch, they have few passing options, and very little chance of breaking past the defence. Try to stagger your players, so you can use diagonal passing up and downfield to give your attack depth and flexibility.

Below, the zigzag spacing of the blue attackers gives their attack depth.

Make sure you stay onside as you push upfield.

USING A CROSS-OVER MOVE

A cross-over move is when you and a team-mate run past each other to confuse your opponents.

A cross-over move can be played with or without the ball. To play one with the ball, dribble across the pitch towards a team-mate who is running in the opposite direction.

As your paths cross, flick the ball across into your team-mate's path. He can take advantage of the defenders' confusion, and the space behind them, to push upfield into attack.

Above, player A looks to pass. B drops back as though to receive the ball, taking his marker with him. Player C 'crosses over' with B, and runs past him to receive the pass from A.

As with a cross-over off the ball, the aim is to draw two defenders together to create space elsewhere on the pitch.

A cross-over move like this is a great way to change the direction of attack suddenly.

COMBINING SKILLS FOR TEAM ATTACK

This is an example of how a team can combine good positioning, intelligent runs off the ball and accurate passing to build an attack and create a chance to score. The move starts with player A on the ball, moving up from midfield.

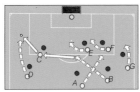

A and B use a cross-over move to switch the attack to C. Player D makes an overlapping run onto a pass from C. E and F draw their markers left.

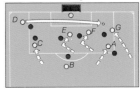

Player G runs into a good striking position, blindside of the defenders, to receive a long cross from D. The other players move up in support.

41

CROSSING TECHNIQUE

If you've built an attack down the wing, you need to get the ball across the front of the opposition goal to give a team-mate the chance to shoot (see page 48) or head for goal (see page 46). Sending a pass from the wing to the centre is known as crossing the ball. Many goals scored in open play come from crosses.

TARGET AREAS

The idea of a cross is to move the ball from the wing, where it is difficult to shoot or score from, into the 'danger area' behind the defence and in front of the goal.

You can use different lengths of cross to create different attacking moves. The three main areas to aim for, shown below, are called the near post, mid-goal and far post areas.

The 'near' and 'far' areas depend which side you're crossing from.

Near post area   Far post area
Mid-goal area

CROSSING TECHNIQUE

To hit a cross, you use the inside of your foot to strike through the lower half of the ball. Strike the ball slightly off-centre. This makes it spin, so that your cross swings into the target area.

Take a good backswing.

Get your non-kicking foot slightly behind and to the side of the ball.

Kick the lower half of the ball to make it rise.

Wrap your foot around the outside of the ball as you kick, to make it spin.

Swing your kicking leg across your body as you follow through.

GETTING IN YOUR CROSS

You need to be able to cross even if an opponent is challenging you.

Push the ball upfield along the wing, past the defender.

You don't need to beat the defender – just create enough space to hit a cross.

Quickly get your cross in before the defender has time to block the ball.

'CHECK-BACK' CROSS MOVE

A 'check-back' is when you stop the ball suddenly. Sprint down the wing as though you mean to cross with the foot nearest the touchline. Stop the ball, and drag it back downfield.

Your check-back will throw your marker. Hit a cross with your other foot, while he is off balance.

CROSSING DRILL

Place two markers as shown. Player A passes to player B, who dribbles along the wing. At the second marker, he crosses the ball to player C.

The players all move round one position, as shown, with player C taking the ball back to the first marker. The sequence then begins again.

★ Vary the position of player C to practise different lengths of cross.

★ Move the second marker for crosses nearer to, or further from the goal-line.

★ Add a defender whose job is to prevent player B getting in his cross.

43

HEADING THE BALL

Controlling the ball with your head is a very important skill to learn, especially if you are playing in attack and want to make the most of a good, high cross into the penalty area. The main points to remember are to keep your eyes open and to use your forehead, not the top of your head. You may find it easier to begin with a fairly light, soft ball.

BASIC HEADING TECHNIQUE

Put yourself in line with the ball. With one foot in front of the other, bend your knees and lean back.

As the ball comes close, try to keep your eyes open. Stay relaxed right up to the last minute.

Attack the ball with your forehead. If you use any other part of your head it can be painful.

Push the ball away, keeping your neck muscles firm so that your head can direct the ball.

POWER HEADING

Put one foot in front of the other for balance and bend your legs as the ball comes towards you.

Keep your eyes fixed on the ball and take off on one foot. This gives you more power and height.

Drive forward as powerfully as you can with your forehead, keeping your eyes open.

Watch where the ball goes as you land so that you are ready to carry out your next move.

CONTROL HEADING

Use a control header to cushion the ball if you want to play the next move yourself instead of passing.

Don't lean quite as far back as the ball approaches. Stay relaxed to provide a cushion for the ball.

Hold your position as you receive the ball. Bend your knees and lean back slightly further.

Push the ball forward gently, so that it drops and lands not far from your feet.

HEADING PRACTICE

Work with a partner. Stand about 4m (13ft) apart. Your partner throws the ball for you to head back. Have five goes at each of these techniques, then swap.

Basic heading

First, cushion the ball with a control header. Let it drop to the ground. Pass it back.

Control heading

Next, head the ball so that your partner can catch it easily.

Power heading

Finally, power the ball away, heading it over your partner.

Make sure you keep your eye on the ball as you head it.

HEADING IN ATTACK

Using headers in attack or to go for goal is one of the most exciting elements of the game. It often means taking advantage of split-second opportunities, so you have to be courageous, take risks and really attack the ball.

DOWNWARD HEADERS

When heading for goal, you should try to keep the ball down to make it more difficult for goalkeepers to save. To make the ball go down when you head it, you need to get above it to hit the top part of it, then nod your head down firmly as you make contact.

1. To catch the top part of the ball with your forehead, you often have to jump.

2. As you would for any header, try to keep your eyes open all the time.

3. As you head the ball away, push forwards and down with your forehead.

DIVING HEADERS

Usually, you use a diving header to try for goal. This is a very dramatic way of scoring, but bear in mind that once you have committed yourself you will be on the ground and unable to play another move until you get up again.

This player watches where the ball has gone. He must now get up quickly in case he needs to follow it up.

Approach a diving header with plenty of speed. This will add to its power.

Keep your eyes on the ball and dive forwards, letting your legs leave the ground.

Direct the ball to the left or right by turning your head as you make contact.

As you hit the ground, try to relax your body so that you don't hurt yourself.

HEADING PRACTICE

This is a practice for three players. Mark out a goal 6m (20ft) across. Place a marker 15m (49ft) in front of it. One player is the goalkeeper.

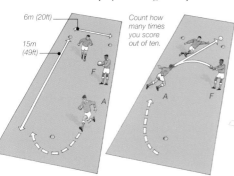

6m (20ft)

15m (49ft)

Count how many times you score out of ten.

One player (F) stands at the side of the goal. The other (A) stands between the goal and the marker. A runs around the marker as F throws the ball to him.

A has to dash for the ball and head at goal. F should vary the height of the ball for A to try different headers. Rotate players after ten goes.

THROW-HEAD-CATCH GAME

This game is for eight or more players. Divide into two teams. Each team has a goal and goalkeeper. Everyone else marks a player from the other team. To play, you must follow the sequence 'throw, head, catch', even when you intercept the ball. You can only score a goal with a header.

FLICK-ON HEADERS

There is one exception to the rule of using your forehead when heading, and that is when you let the ball glance off the top of your head. You usually do this to lift the ball out of the reach of a defender, to a team-mate who may be able to shoot.

As the ball passes over you, jump straight into the air and let it glance off your head. It carries on in basically the same direction, though you can direct it left or right slightly.

SHOOTING

Soccer is all about scoring goals and being able to shoot will give you a great chance of doing this. But shooting is about tactics as well as technique. When you decide to shoot, you need to pick the most vulnerable part of the goal, and the best approach to beat the goalkeeper.

PICKING YOUR TARGET

Always try to keep your shot low. It's far harder for a goalkeeper to reach down from a standing position to cover a low shot than it is for him to stretch to reach a high one.

The further your shot is from the goalkeeper, the harder it will be for him to reach the ball. Aim just inside whichever post is furthest away from the goalkeeper.

Follow your shot in. If it rebounds from the goalkeeper, post or crossbar, you may get another chance to score.

Accuracy is more important than power – carefully pushing the ball past the goalkeeper is better than blasting it wildly at goal.

LONG RANGE SHOTS

Don't hesitate to shoot from a long way out because you're worried that your team-mates will blame you if you miss. The more shots you try, the more likely your team is to score. Bear in mind that players between you and the goal may block the goalkeeper's view, or even deflect your shot, making it harder to save.

A good striker shoots whenever he gets the chance. It's better to try for a goal and miss than not to try at all.

BEATING THE KEEPER

A goalkeeper will reduce the area you can aim at by moving out towards you as you approach goal (see page 88).

Here there are large areas on either side of the keeper to aim at.

By moving off his goal-line, the goalkeeper reduces the target areas.

If the goalkeeper 'narrows the angle' like this, and you think he is likely to block a shot to either side, try dribbling the ball past him instead.

1. You need to make the goalkeeper commit himself. Make as though to shoot past him so that he 'spreads' to block the ball.

2. Once he is on the ground, take the ball past him, or chip it over him. Run on and aim the ball carefully into the goal.

WHEN NOT TO SHOOT

However good your shooting skills are, you will sometimes find that your angle of approach and the defenders in your path mean that you've little chance of scoring. If you can see that one of your team-mates is in a better position, pass the ball to him.

The referee tosses a coin to decide which team kicks off.

CENTRE KICKS

Every soccer match begins with a centre kick, called the 'kick-off'. It gives you an early chance to take control of the ball. Centre kicks are also used to get the second half underway, to restart the game whenever a team scores a goal, and to begin any periods of extra time.

Wait for the referee to blow his whistle before you take the kick.

CENTRE KICK RULES

All centre kicks are taken from the centre spot. When you take the kick, every player must be in his own half. Once you've struck the ball, you mustn't kick it again until it has been touched by another player. You can score straight from the centre spot.

Opposition players must be outside the centre circle when you take the kick.

You have to play the ball forwards from the spot, into the other team's half.

A SHORT, SAFE CENTRE KICK

A centre kick gives you possession of the ball in midfield. To keep possession, so that you can control play, use a short pass to a team-mate standing alongside you in the centre circle.

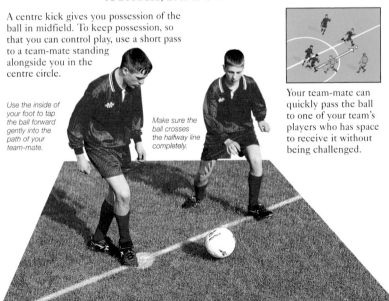

Use the inside of your foot to tap the ball forward gently into the path of your team-mate.

Make sure the ball crosses the halfway line completely.

Your team-mate can quickly pass the ball to one of your team's players who has space to receive it without being challenged.

PRESSURING THE OPPOSITION

You can use a longer centre kick to move play upfield quickly and put pressure on the other team.

Kick the ball upfield into the attacking third. Aim for a space behind the other team's midfield players.

Your attacking players should sprint upfield from the halfway line to challenge for possession.

This tactic might well cause your team to lose the ball, but it can sometimes create an early scoring chance.

STAR CENTRE

Here, the Greek national team kick-off against Portugal in Lisbon. They opt for a short centre kick in order to keep possession of the ball. At the bottom of the picture, a Greek attacker makes an early run into the Portuguese half of the pitch to help start an attack.

CREATING AN OVERLOAD

If you decide to try a long centre kick, your team will have a better chance of winning the ball if several of your players gather on one side of the pitch.

Angle your kick to the 'overloaded' side of the pitch, into the path of your attacking players.

The other team may realize what you are planning, and move across to the overloaded side of the pitch.

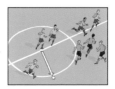

In this case, try switching your centre kick move at the last minute, playing the ball to the other side.

THROW-IN TECHNIQUE

If an opposition player knocks the ball over either touchline, one of your team's players has to throw it back onto the pitch. This is known as taking a throw-in. It is the only type of restart which involves using your hands to bring the ball back into play.

A referee's assistant points his flag to signal a throw-in.

The team playing in the direction of the flag takes the throw.

THROW-IN RULES

To throw the ball back into play you have to bring it forwards from behind your head, using both hands. As you release the ball, part of both your feet must be touching the ground, on or behind the touchline.

You cannot score a goal by throwing the ball straight into the opposition's goal.

HOW TO HOLD THE BALL

Make sure that you hold the ball with your fingers spread around its back and sides. Your thumbs should nearly touch.

Feet on ground, on or behind touchline.

Holding the ball like this lets you control it more easily as you release your throw.

PRACTISING YOUR THROW-IN

You need to be able to throw accurately or you may give away the ball. To improve your throw, try this exercise with a partner.

Stand about 10m (33ft) apart. Use throw-ins to pass the ball back and forth. Throw the ball to your partner's feet so that he can control it easily.

As you get better at throwing the ball, your partner can give you a specific target area. Try throwing to your partner's head, chest and thigh.

TAKING A LONGER THROW-IN

Most professional soccer teams have at least one player who specializes in throwing the ball a long way. Practise the technique shown here to develop a long, accurate throw-in.

Arch your back to bring the ball as far back as possible.

Place your leading foot close behind the touchline.

At least part of your trailing foot must be touching the ground.

Use your hands and fingers to direct the ball's flight.

Leading leg

Hold the ball in front of your head and take a couple of quick steps towards the touchline.

Take a long final stride to reach the line, bringing the ball right back behind your head.

With the weight on your leading leg, whip the upper part of your body forwards to catapult the ball away.

THROWING AWAY POSSESSION

If you break one of the rules when you take a throw-in, the referee will ask the other team to retake the throw. Take care not to give away possession with a foul throw. The pictures below show the things you need to avoid to keep your throw-in legal.

FOUL THROW - The player's feet are too far over the touchline for a legal throw-in.

FOUL THROW - The thrower's right foot is off the ground as he releases the ball.

FOUL THROW - The player hasn't brought the ball far enough back over his head.

STAR THROW

Here, Gabriel Heinze, playing for Manchester United, prepares to launch a throw-in along the wing.

CORNER KICKS

When a defending player hits the ball over his own goal-line, the referee awards the attacking team a corner kick. This gives you a chance to play the ball across the opposition's goalmouth for a team-mate to strike at goal.

To signal a corner, the referee points to the corner flag.

You have to take a corner kick with the corner flag in position.

CORNER KICK RULES

To take a corner, you kick the ball from within the corner quarter circle nearest to the point where it went out of play.

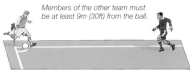

Members of the other team must be at least 9m (30ft) from the ball.

You're not allowed to play the ball again until another player has touched it.

PLACING THE BALL FOR A CORNER KICK

You need to place the ball in the corner circle in such a way that you can kick it without the flag blocking your run up or swing. The best place to put the ball will depend on whether you are left- or right-footed.

Here, the ball is placed correctly for a left-footed corner kicker.

Here, the ball is placed correctly for a right-footed corner kicker.

CROSSING FROM THE CORNER

If you hit a long, lofted corner kick to a team-mate just beyond the far side of the goal, he'll have a chance to shoot from behind the goalkeeper's view.

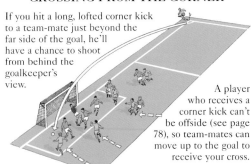

A player who receives a corner kick can't be offside (see page 78), so team-mates can move up to the goal to receive your cross.

INSWINGERS

You can make your cross even more effective by bending it, so that the ball swings in towards the goal. A corner kick like this is known as an inswinger.

HOW DO YOU BEND A CORNER KICK?

The secret to bending a corner kick cross is to strike the ball off-centre so that it spins as it travels through the air. The easiest way to do this is to use the inside of your kicking foot to strike the outside edge of the ball. This right-footed player is about to hit an inswinger from the left corner in this way.

You also need to remember to hit the ball below its midline, so that your cross has plenty of lift.

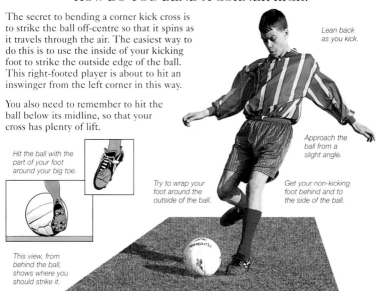

Lean back as you kick.

Approach the ball from a slight angle.

Hit the ball with the part of your foot around your big toe.

Try to wrap your foot around the outside of the ball.

Get your non-kicking foot behind and to the side of the ball.

This view, from behind the ball, shows where you should strike it.

PRACTISING YOUR CROSS

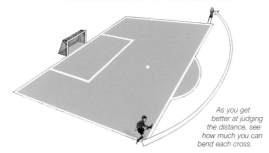

As you get better at judging the distance, see how much you can bend each cross.

Try this practice with a partner to get used to the length and height of a good cross. Stand on the front corners of the penalty area – or about 40m (130ft) apart if you're not on a pitch. This is about the distance from the corner to the farthest post. Hit crosses to one another, trying to deliver the ball so that your partner can catch it just above his head.

WHO KICKS?

Bending a kick using the inside of your foot makes the ball swing away to the left if you're right-footed, or to the right if you're left-footed. Make sure that you pick the correct player to take an inswinger from a particular side of the pitch.

A right-footed player takes inswingers from left of the goal.

A left-footed player takes inswingers from right of the goal.

CORNER KICK MOVES

A cross from the corner is an example of a 'fifty-fifty' ball, as both teams have an equal chance of gaining possession. You can tip the balance in your team's favour by using a pre-planned corner move. These two pages suggest several corner kick routines for you to try.

FINDING SPACE TO RECEIVE A CROSS

For any corner kick move to be successful, one of your team-mates in the penalty area needs to be free to receive the ball and shoot. As you prepare to take a corner, your attacking players should try to move away from defenders to find space.

Here, the blue attacking players are getting ready to receive a cross from the right-hand corner.

The blue players in the far side of the penalty area can strike from a long cross or a flicked-on ball (see below).

This blue player is trying to find space to receive a shorter, driven cross.

There is a good chance for a shot into this side of the goal, which the red team has left unguarded.

FROM THE NEAR POST TO THE FAR POST

For this move, one of your team-mates needs to move into space around the goal-post nearest to the corner that you are kicking from. This post is called the 'near post'. Send a short, inswinging cross to

this player. He then uses his head to flick the ball on across the goal. One of your other team-mates runs in on the far side of the goal area, close to the 'far post', to receive the ball and shoot.

Judge your cross so that your team-mate can head the ball.

LAYING THE BALL BACK

This alternative near post move can be as effective as a flick-on across the goal. Send a cross to a team-mate at the near post. Instead of heading the ball across the goalmouth, the receiver 'lays it back'.

This means heading it down into the path of a team-mate running in from midfield.

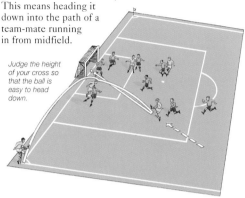

Judge the height of your cross so that the ball is easy to head down.

OUTSWINGING CORNERS

Another option is to bend your corner kick cross away from the goalmouth. This kind of corner is called an 'outswinger'. It makes it easier for your team-mates moving towards goal to head the ball well.

Players can run onto your cross from the edge of the penalty area.

Play your cross so that the ball swings out towards the penalty spot.

By moving out towards the corner, or over towards the far post, your team-mates can draw defenders away from the near side of the penalty area. This creates space for a player to run onto a shorter outswinging cross.

This player is drawing away a defender to create space.

CORNER ACTION

Try to spot different corner moves when you watch players in action. Here, Manchester United and England star Wayne Rooney is deciding what type of corner move to try. His team-mates will try to head the ball into the goal.

WHO KICKS?

As with inswingers (see page 55), you need to pick the correct kicker to take an outswinging corner from a particular side of the pitch.

A right-footed player takes outswinging corners from the right-hand side of the goal.

A left-footed player takes outswinging corners from the left-hand side of the goal.

FREE KICK BASICS

The referee puts his arm out to signal a direct free kick.

If one of your opponents 'commits an offence' by breaking a soccer rule, the referee will stop the game and ask your team to restart play with a free kick. There are two types of free kick – direct, to punish serious offences, and indirect for less serious ones.

To signal an indirect free kick, the referee raises his arm.

SERIOUS OFFENCES

The referee will award a direct free kick if a player kicks, trips, charges, strikes, pushes, holds or jumps at an opponent; if an outfield player deliberately uses his hands to control the ball, or if a goalkeeper handles the ball outside his penalty area.

Here, the player in yellow is holding his opponent back, rather than playing the ball. An unfair challenge like this is known as a foul.

If a player commits a direct free kick offence like this in his own penalty area, the referee will award the other team a penalty kick (see page 58).

INDIRECT FREE KICK OFFENCES

These pictures show some of the most common offences for which a referee will award an indirect free kick. The offences in the top row are all to do with goalkeepers.

Obstructing the opposition's goalkeeper.

Using hands to receive a backpass from a team-mate.

Holding the ball for more than six seconds.

All players need to be very careful not to give away indirect free kicks. They give the opposing team the chance to build a dangerous attack on goal.

Playing dangerously (here, kicking a high ball).

Obstructing a player who isn't on the ball.

Receiving the ball while in an offside position (see page 72).

FREE KICK RULES

To take a free kick, you kick the ball from the point on the pitch where the offence took place. The ball must be stationary when you kick it, and the other team's players have to be at least 9m (30ft) away. You can't play the ball again until it has been touched by another player.

If the free kick is direct, you are allowed to score straight from the kick.

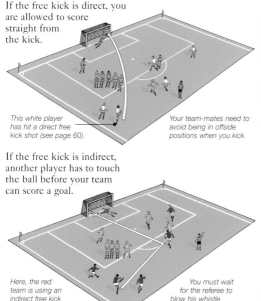

This white player has hit a direct free kick shot (see page 60).

Your team-mates need to avoid being in offside positions when you kick.

If the free kick is indirect, another player has to touch the ball before your team can score a goal.

Here, the red team is using an indirect free kick move.

You must wait for the referee to blow his whistle before you take the kick.

SPECIAL CASES

If you are awarded a free kick in your own penalty area, you have to kick the ball out of the penalty area to bring it back into play.

Opposition players must be outside the penalty area when you kick.

If the kick is inside your goal area, you can take it from any part of that area.

If you are given an indirect free kick inside your opponent's goal area, you take the kick from the edge of the goal area.

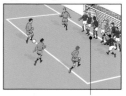

Your opponents are allowed to stand on their goal-line, between the posts, despite being less than 9m (30ft) away.

TAKING A FREE KICK IN YOUR OWN HALF

The top priority when you take a free kick in your own half of the pitch is to make sure that your team keeps the ball. Use a simple pass to a player in space.

Aim your kick away from any nearby opponent hoping to steal the ball.

Send the ball upfield whenever possible.

DIRECT FREE KICKS

A free kick in the attacking third gives you a good chance to score a spectacular goal. You're most likely to score if you keep your free kick move simple. These pages look at the simplest of all attacking free kicks – a direct shot at goal from the edge of the penalty area.

THE DEFENSIVE WALL

When you take a free kick near the penalty area, your opponents will usually protect their goalmouth by forming a defensive wall. Several players will stand side by side to block your shooting line. To score, you need to get the ball past this wall of players.

The players in the wall will try to block one side of the goalmouth, while their goalkeeper guards the other.

BENDING YOUR SHOT AROUND THE WALL

By striking the outside edge of the ball with the inside of your foot, you can bend a free kick so that it swings away to your non-kicking side. Don't hit the ball too low down or it will rise over the goal.

To bend a kick in the other direction, so that it swings out to your kicking side, use the outside of your foot to strike the inside edge of the ball. Keep the toes of your kicking foot pointed down as you kick.

Here, a right-footed player is bending a free kick shot around the wall.

To do this, the player hits this area of the ball with the inside of his foot.

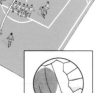

Here, a right-footed player is bending a shot in the other direction.

To do this, the player hits this area of the ball with the outside of his foot.

BENDING SHOT PRACTICE

To practise your swerving shot, put one corner flag in the centre of the goal, and another on the penalty spot. Place the ball on the penalty arc, in line with the flags. Try to bend a kick around one side of the nearest flag into the other side of the goalmouth.

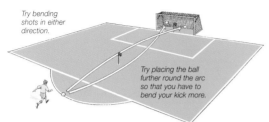

Try bending shots in either direction.

Try placing the ball further round the arc so that you have to bend your kick more.

SHOOTING STAR

Here, a Japanese player is trying to bend a powerful, left-footed free kick at the goal. His Indian opponents have formed a wall in front of their goal.

USING A DUMMY CROSS-OVER

You can use this tactic to disguise the direction of a direct free kick shot.

1. You and a team-mate (ideally a player who kicks with the opposite foot to you) both prepare as though to take the kick.

2. Your team-mate runs up to the ball, as though to shoot, but steps over it at the last minute.

Your team-mate's run will help to hide your shot.

3. Time your own run up so that just after your team-mate 'dummies' over the ball, you hit a powerful shot at goal. Your team-mate can continue his run to follow in your shot.

PENALTIES

To signal a penalty, the referee points at the penalty spot.

When a player commits a serious offence inside his own penalty area, the referee awards the attacking team a penalty kick. A penalty is a high-pressure, 'one-on-one' situation in which you try to beat the opposition's goalkeeper with a direct shot at goal.

Place the ball yourself, so that you know it is on a sound surface.

PENALTY RULES

To take a penalty, you shoot at goal from the penalty spot. You can't play the ball again until it has been touched by another player.

The goalkeeper must stay on the goal-line before you shoot.

All other players must be outside the penalty area, beyond the arc, and downfield from the spot.

STAYING COOL

When you take a penalty, don't be indecisive or hesitant. Pick your target area and concentrate on hitting a hard, low shot into that part of the goal.

A firmly hit shot just inside either post will be extremely hard to stop.

SHOOTING WITH POWER

1. The key to a low, hard shot is to keep your body over the ball as you kick, rather than leaning back.

2. Get your non-kicking foot alongside the ball so that the knee of your kicking leg is over the ball.

3. With your toes pointing down, use the instep of your kicking foot to drive the ball forward.

Use your arms for balance.

Follow through with your kicking leg for maximum power.

Strike the ball through its midline, so that it stays low.

SOFT OPTION

You may find it easier to place your shot accurately by hitting the ball with slightly less power, using the inside of your foot.

FOLLOWING UP THE PENALTY

Your team-mates should be ready to close in on the goalmouth as soon as you've taken your penalty kick.

If the goalkeeper blocks your shot, the ball may rebound to provide another chance.

THE PENALTY SHOOT-OUT

If the scores are level at the end of a match, the teams sometimes have a penalty competition to decide which team wins. This is known as a penalty 'shoot-out'. If one team has scored more goals after both teams have had five penalty attempts, then that team wins the match. Otherwise, the shoot-out continues until one team's penalty score passes the other team's from the same number of attempts.

These players are using a practice penalty shoot-out in training to perfect their penalty skills.

In a shoot-out, each penalty has to be taken by a different player, so every member of your team needs to practise.

A practice shoot-out will also improve your goalkeeper's skills.

DEFENDING

A team can't use a bold attack unless it can depend on a solid defence. Read here about how to challenge your opponents effectively, use tactics like the offside trap, and improve your goalkeeping skills.

PRIORITIES IN DEFENCE

The main purpose of a defender or defending team is to stop opponents from attacking. There are many ways to do this, depending on how urgent the situation is. To be successful, a team must have a strong defence. Here, you can find out about the most important things you need to know.

YOUR TOP PRIORITY

If your opponents reach the defending third, they are in a very strong position. You must stop them from scoring.

First, help your goalkeeper to block any shots at goal. Next, clear the ball out of the danger area – 'if in doubt, get the ball out.'

Here, a defender stops a shot and clears the ball.

CHALLENGING FOR THE BALL

Whatever the situation, someone must try to win the ball back. This responsibility passes from player to player, so everyone must be ready to take on the challenge if the ball comes his way.

Attacker — *Defender*

You can challenge by putting pressure on the player with the ball.

If your opponent makes a mistake, you or a team-mate can intercept the ball.

As a last resort, you can challenge your opponent directly with a tackle.

DELAYING YOUR OPPONENTS

A very important way of preventing an emergency situation from happening is to delay your opponents as long as possible.

Delaying, or jockeying (see page 68), allows team-mates to get into a strong position, from which they can stop an attack.

This player jockeys to give a team-mate time to get into position.

AWARENESS AND TEAM WORK

Even if one player's skills are very good, he will not stand a very big chance of challenging for the ball successfully if his team is not working with him.

Each player has a part to play in making it difficult for the other team to progress up the field. To do this you need to communicate well.

Everyone needs to be aware of where the ball is, but not everyone should crowd around it.

All players should be aware of what the attackers are doing, especially the players they are marking.

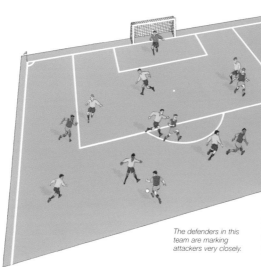

The defenders in this team are marking attackers very closely.

Each player needs to understand his team's formation and how his own position works within it.

DEFENCE INTO ATTACK

If you only think about stopping the other team from scoring, you are less likely to score yourself. A good defence makes the whole team strong, but it should always be used as a springboard for attack.

Think positively all the time so that you can turn defensive situations into an attack as soon as you get the chance.

This team gains possession in the defending third, then sends the ball quickly up the pitch.

STAR DEFENDER

Spanish star Asier Del Horno is a good example of a defender who can read the game well, then act courageously to turn defence into attack.

JOCKEYING

Jockeying is one of the most important defending skills. It means delaying your opponent's attack by getting in his way. This allows your team-mates to get into a position where they can help you to challenge. If you do this effectively, you may also pressurize your opponent into making a mistake.

MOVING INTO POSITION

If your opponent is approaching your goal you need to close in on him quickly, but not too quickly. If you are going too fast he will be able to judge your run and dodge round you easily.

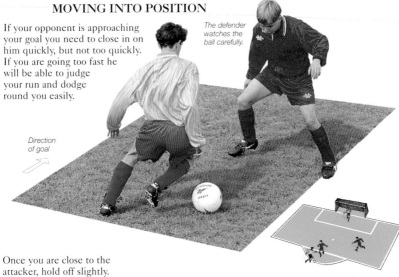

The defender watches the ball carefully.

Direction of goal

Once you are close to the attacker, hold off slightly. You should be close enough to touch him, but if you get much closer it will be easy for him to dash round you.

Keep your body well balanced. If your weight is over your knees, you are in a good position to challenge.

Make sure you block the path to goal. If the attacker gets round you, you will no longer be able to jockey.

MAINTAINING THE PRESSURE

As well as delaying your opponent, try to force him into a weaker position. First of all, try to work out which is his weaker side – if he usually uses his right foot to dribble or kick, he is weak on his left side.

This player jockeys on the left.

Cover your opponent to the front and to one side so that it is difficult for him to turn.

The attacker is forced into the side-lines.

If you jockey on his strong side, he will only be able to use his weak side, so he may make a mistake.

Here, the attacker loses the initiative.

Once you have your opponent under pressure, watch for opportunities to win the ball.

68

PREVENTING A FULL TURN

If the attacker is still facing away from your goal when you reach a jockeying position, you have a big advantage. The best thing you can do is prevent him from turning.

1. Jockey on his stronger side, getting close up behind him. Make sure you don't come round to his front.

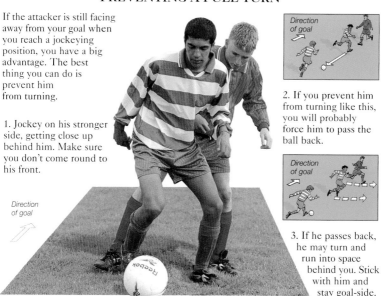

Direction of goal

2. If you prevent him from turning like this, you will probably force him to pass the ball back.

Direction of goal

3. If he passes back, he may turn and run into space behind you. Stick with him and stay goal-side.

ZIGZAG JOCKEYING EXERCISE

This exercise helps you to work on speed and a good defensive stance. Any number can join in, as long as you work in pairs. Mark out a row of zigzags about 30m (98ft) long and 5m (16ft) wide. One end of the row is the defender's goal. In each pair, decide on an attacker and a defender.

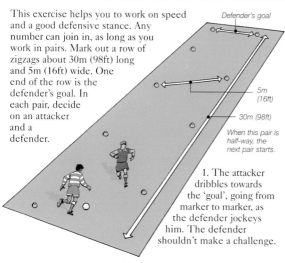

Defender's goal

5m (16ft)

30m (98ft)

When this pair is half-way, the next pair starts.

1. The attacker dribbles towards the 'goal', going from marker to marker, as the defender jockeys him. The defender shouldn't make a challenge.

2. The defender can't tackle, but he scores a point for intercepting the ball if the attacker loses control. The attacker scores if he dodges round the defender. At the end of the row, swap roles and start again.

CHALLENGING

When you challenge, you make a direct attempt to get the ball back from your opponents. The most direct way to challenge is to tackle, but it is not always the best. If you can intercept the ball instead, do so, because this will leave you with more control.

Defender

APPROACHING AN OPPONENT

You usually move in to challenge when your opponent is about to receive a pass. Always get into a goal-side position.

The defender should not run right to the back of his opponent in the direction of the curved arrow.

Approach your opponent at an angle. If you are directly behind him, he can easily run out to the side.

Don't get in too close to him, as he may be able to dodge round you.

Judge your speed carefully. If you come in too slowly he may run on. If you are too fast, you have less control.

This defender has come in too fast and too close. He is off balance.

If the defender approaches in this direction, he will be able to challenge the attacker.

Direction of goal

INTERCEPTING

Intercepting is the best way to win the ball back. Your opponents are usually moving in the wrong direction, and you are more balanced than if you tackle. This means that you have time and space to launch an attack.

Be patient and wait for a chance to intercept. Attackers may make mistakes under pressure.

You must be on your toes and ready to dash around your opponent from your goal-side position.

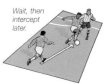

Wait, then intercept later.

If you don't think you can intercept successfully, hold on to your goal-side position instead.

TIMING A DIRECT CHALLENGE

If you are close to your opponent, you will probably need to tackle in order to win the ball. In judging your tackle, the most important factor is timing.

One of the main rules of timing is to watch the ball, not the player. This way, you won't be fooled by his movements. Wait until he is off balance, for example when he is turning or half-turned, then move in quickly to steal the ball. You can find out more about tackling techniques on pages 72-73.

As this player turns with the ball, the defender dashes across the front of him and pushes the ball away.

INTERCEPTING EXERCISE

This exercise is to help you develop your agility and speed at intercepting. Play in threes (A, B and D). Mark out a 10m (33ft) square. A and D stand in the middle of it, B along one edge. The direction of play is towards A and D.

D stands goal-side of A. B passes towards them. D must judge whether to intercept or stay goal-side.

If D intercepts, he scores a point and passes the ball back to B before A can challenge him.

If A gets the ball, D tries to stop him reaching the far side of the square before B can count to ten.

A scores a point for turning and reaching the other side. After five goes, swap your roles around.

TACKLING SKILLS

To tackle well you need a combination of good technique and plenty of determination. You need to tackle cleanly to avoid giving away a foul, and whenever possible you need to keep possession of the ball, too. These are the main techniques that you need to learn.

FRONT BLOCK TACKLE

Watch the ball, not your opponent. With your weight forward, go into the tackle with your whole body.

Use the inside of your tackling foot to make contact with the middle of the ball.

If you watch your opponent instead of the ball, you may be tricked by a feinting move.

The impact of the tackle can often trap the ball between your foot and your opponent's foot. If this happens, drop your foot down and try to flick or roll the ball up over your opponent's foot.

TACKLING FROM OTHER ANGLES

You can use a block tackle to challenge from the side, but not from behind as this is a foul.

Turn your whole body towards your opponent so that all your strength is behind the tackle. Use the side of your tackling foot as you would if you were face on. Lean into your opponent, but don't push.

BLOCK TACKLE PRACTICE

In pairs, mark out a 10m (33ft) line. Start at either end. One player dribbles, the other challenges.

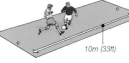

10m (33ft)

The dribbler tries to get to the end of the line, while the challenger tries to win the ball from him. Whoever succeeds scores a point.

SLIDING TACKLES

Sliding tackles are a last resort. You should only use them in a real emergency, for several reasons. You will probably not gain possession of the ball, you are out of the game until you get up again, and you may also give away a foul.

Approach from the side. Keep your eyes on the ball and slide your tackling leg forward to push the ball as far as possible.

This player uses the leg furthest from his opponent to hook the ball away from him.

If you kick the ball and not your opponent, you will not be penalised if he has to jump over you.

After tackling, get up quickly. This is easier if you tackle with the leg furthest from your opponent.

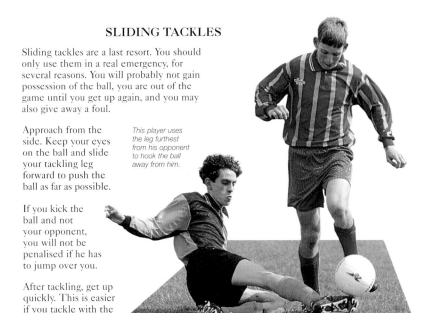

LEARNING TO SLIDE TACKLE

Until you are sure of your technique, it is best to practise sliding tackles without an opponent, as you are less likely to hurt someone. Try this practice with a friend.

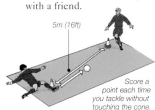

5m (16ft)

Score a point each time you tackle without touching the cone.

Place two obstacles 5m (16ft) apart (they needn't be cones) and put the ball close to one of them. These are your 'opponents'. Each of you starts next to an obstacle.

One of you runs up and slides the ball away, trying not to touch the obstacle. The other collects the ball and puts it next to his own obstacle. He slides it back.

KEEPING IT CLEAN

Tackling your opponent from behind, kicking him or tripping him are fouls which lead to a direct free kick, or a penalty if you are in the penalty area. To avoid fouling, remember these tips:
★ Keep your eyes on the ball, not on your opponent.
★ Be patient. If you wait for the right moment to make a tackle, you are more likely to do so cleanly.
★ Never tackle half-heartedly. If your weight is not behind the tackle, you may be unbalanced, and you could hurt yourself as well as your opponent.

MARKING SYSTEMS

A marking system is a way of organising your team so that everyone knows who should be covering which attacker. These are the systems used most often, which can be adapted to fit the strengths and weaknesses of your team.

MAN-TO-MAN MARKING

When your team marks man-to-man, a specific defender marks each of the attackers from the other team. They watch this attacker throughout the game and stay goal-side of him whenever necessary.

Here, the defenders are moving into position.

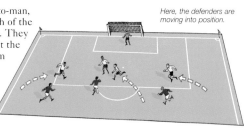

Playing man-to-man works well in the defending third, as long as you have some spare defenders to put the attackers under pressure. Never let just one player mark the opponent who has the ball.

As the play moves across the pitch towards the penalty area, the marking defenders stay with the same player, keeping goal-side and marking tightly. This makes it difficult for the attackers to shoot.

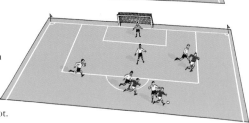

ZONAL MARKING

In zonal marking, you are responsible for an area or zone instead of one player. This area depends on the position you are playing, but not too strictly. As you move up and down the pitch, your area moves with you. Usually, you mark anyone who comes within 5-10m (16-33ft) of you.

In this example of how the zonal system works, an attacker (A) moves across the defence.

D1 covers the player until he moves out of his area, when D2 covers him instead.

The advantage of this is that D1 has not left a big space behind him for attackers to fill.

74

MIXING SYSTEMS

Many professional teams don't work with just one system. Often, they mix different systems to make the most of their skills. This takes a lot of discipline and organization to put into practice effectively.

When one player in the other team is very skilful, one defender might mark him man-to-man while the others mark zonally, as this picture shows.

One defender marks this fast winger closely, while the other defenders mark zonally.

Some teams play zonally in the attacking third and midfield, then use a man-to-man system in defence.

You can also mark different players at different times as a looser man-to-man system.

USING A SWEEPER

Whichever system you use, it is too risky to allow a one-on-one situation to develop in the defending third. To stop this from happening, you can use a 'sweeper', who doesn't mark anyone (see page 77). He stays at the back and 'sweeps up' attackers who get past the main defence.

FINDING THE BEST SYSTEM

There is no 'best system' which works for every team in every situation. These are the factors which are important.

★ Whatever system you use, the whole team must fully understand it. Each player must know exactly what he is supposed to do.

★ Try to find out about your opponents and about their strengths and weaknesses. If they have some good players, make sure they are well marked.

★ Think about the skills of your own team – for example, you might put a row of strong players to mark zonally at the back, and you wouldn't place a weak player man-to-man against a strong opponent.

This sweeper gets into a good position to challenge an attacker who has broken through the defence.

Direction of goal

TEAM FORMATIONS

Along with a marking system, each professional team has a formation. A formation is almost like a map of the positions that the players stick to during the game. It can be different each time a team plays, though teams often use the one they feel most confident with.

HOW IS A FORMATION BUILT?

A strong formation always has a strong defence. A team is usually built up solidly with a strong group of defenders at the back for the attackers to rely upon. The idea is that if the other team can't score, they can't win. This way of thinking, however, can lead to play that is too defensive and to games which end in a draw. To win, teams also need to give the midfield and attackers support and freedom to push forward and score, so modern formations are designed for this as well.

FOUR-FOUR-TWO

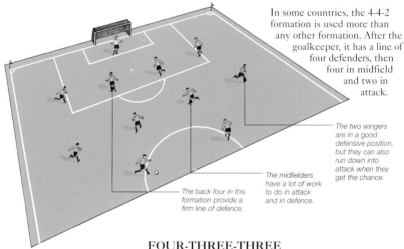

In some countries, the 4-4-2 formation is used more than any other formation. After the goalkeeper, it has a line of four defenders, then four in midfield and two in attack.

The two wingers are in a good defensive position, but they can also run down into attack when they get the chance.

The midfielders have a lot of work to do in attack and in defence.

The back four in this formation provide a firm line of defence.

FOUR-THREE-THREE

This formation is similar to the 4-4-2 formation. It has a goalkeeper, four defenders, three midfielders and three attackers. The advantage of this is that there is more emphasis on attack, but if a team comes under pressure, it can quickly change to 4-5-1 with just one attacker and extra midfielders.

Having less midfielders can weaken a defence.

THE SWEEPER FORMATION

Using a sweeper changes a formation at the back. Traditionally, the system is based on a five-man defence. The usual line of four is backed up by a 'spare' man or sweeper.

This formation gives a very secure defence. However, with so many players at the back, a team using it may find it difficult to attack.

Another version has more players in attack. It uses the usual back four, but one player drops back when necessary to play sweeper.

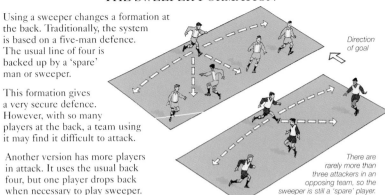

Direction of goal

There are rarely more than three attackers in an opposing team, so the sweeper is still a 'spare' player.

OTHER FORMATIONS

There are many other combinations which teams can try. This is an example. It is based on the 4-4-2 formation, but it is a lot more flexible.

This system has a 'link' player between the defence and midfield, and between the midfield and attack. In defence, the 'link' is similar to a sweeper but in front of the line of backs instead of behind them.

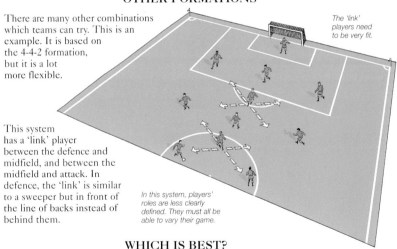

The 'link' players need to be very fit.

In this system, players' roles are less clearly defined. They must all be able to vary their game.

WHICH IS BEST?

Each formation has its advantages and teams tend to get used to playing in one way. Many European teams, for example, use a sweeper. The following factors make a difference when you are deciding which to use.

★ Don't try to fit players to a formation which doesn't suit them. Choose one which suits their skills.
★ If you use a very traditional formation, your game may be too easy for your opponents to read.

★ If you use a new, flexible formation, you must all be able to read the game well, and you must also be very fit.
★ Make sure you have a strong defence. If it is weak, you may lose even if your attackers are good.

THE OFFSIDE RULE

The offside rule can sometimes be very useful for defenders, as attackers who are caught in this position have an indirect free kick awarded against them. Here you can find out about how the rule works and the best way for defenders to use it.

OFFSIDE

To be penalized for offside, an attacker must be in your half of the pitch and there must be fewer than two defenders between him and the goal-line. One of these defenders can be the goalkeeper. It is not always illegal to be offside, but it is in any of these cases:

1. A player can only be called offside when the ball is played, not when it is received.

2. Offside should be called if a player's offside position gives him an advantage, for example a chance to shoot.

3. If a player is offside and obstructs a defender to stop him from reaching the ball, he should be penalized.

LEGAL POSITIONS

An attacker will not be penalized for offside in any of these situations:

1. If one of the last defenders is level with him when the ball is passed. To be offside he must be closer to the goal-line.

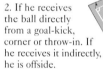

2. If he receives the ball directly from a goal-kick, corner or throw-in. If he receives it indirectly, he is offside.

3. If he runs into an offside position after the ball has been played, or if he dribbles into an offside position.

4. If he is offside, but not interfering with play at all – for example, if he is on the other side of the pitch or if he is lying injured.

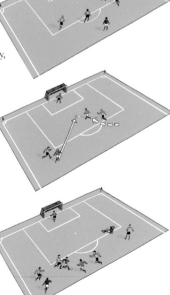

USING OFFSIDE IN DEFENCE

You may see professional defenders trying to place an attacker offside by moving up the pitch together, just at the point when another attacker passes to him. Here you can see how this 'trap' works.

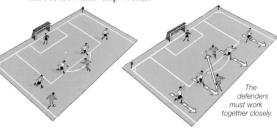

The back line of defenders see that an attacker is about to receive a pass.

They all move up the pitch just before or just as the pass is made.

The defenders must work together closely.

DISADVANTAGES OF USING OFFSIDE

A big problem with using offside is that you depend upon the referee. If he does not call offside, you leave your defence in a very weak position. Also, the trap may not work. If an attacker manages to dribble past you instead of passing, he can go straight for goal.

Which of these situations show a player in an offside position? Think carefully before you decide. The answers are on page 96.

1.

2.

3.

4.

The defenders have all moved up, so it will be difficult for them to help the goalkeeper defend against the attacker.

This attacker fools the defence by dribbling past them instead of passing.

The defenders expect the ball to be passed to this player.

COMMUNICATION

Communicating with your team on the pitch is essential. Many defensive mix-ups and breakdowns in attack are due to a lack of communication. Calls should be clear, concise and calm. Calling for the ball is a special skill. Only call when you're free. You can work on this by playing a five-a-side game where you can only receive a pass if you've called for it. If you don't call, but receive the ball, possession passes to the other side.

SOME COMMON CALLS AND SIGNALS

Always try to use your team-mate's name when shouting 'leave', 'mine', 'time' or 'man-on'. This will prevent any chance of your team-mate not realising who you are shouting at.

'Man-On!' – *tells the on-ball player that an opposing player is approaching. Adding which side the player is coming from is even more helpful.*

'Time' – *tells a player about to receive or on the ball that he is unmarked and has space to turn and view the situation.*

'Leave' or **'Mine'** – *tells a team-mate that you will take the ball.*

'Force him outside' – *is a defensive order meaning stay inside the attacker forcing him towards the touchline.*

Some signals are non-verbal. Here you can see a player signalling to his defence to push up quickly.

A team may have a range of free kicks which they have worked on in training. This player is signalling to his team-mates which sort of free kick he intends to take.

HEAD UP

Communication is not just about what you say or signal, it's also about being in a position to see what your team-mates are doing and saying. For this, you need to have your head up and be aware of the game around you at all times. This is especially important when you are the player in control of the ball.

English international Steven Gerrard has the ball at his feet, but is looking up to spot where his team-mates are placed and what passes are possible.

FIVE V TWO MINI GAME

This fun game helps communication skills. A team of two players act as defenders. They must try to get the ball from the team of five. The team with the ball are each numbered from one to five. One can only pass to two, two to three and so on. If player five manages to pass to player one, the team scores a point. Swap the defenders over once the side has scored three points.

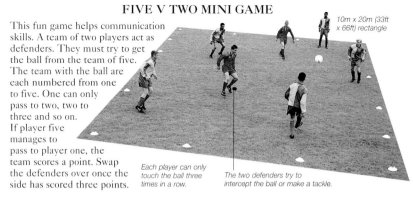

10m x 20m (33ft x 66ft) rectangle

Each player can only touch the ball three times in a row.

The two defenders try to intercept the ball or make a tackle.

THE REFEREE'S SIGNALS

The referee and his two assistants are in charge of the game. Don't argue with them. It doesn't help you or your team. Talking back may earn a yellow, or even a red card. Play until you hear the whistle.

Don't assume that a referee has seen a foul and stop playing. In the noise of a big game, it's not always possible to hear what the referee has said, so it's useful to know his signals.

Hand ball foul
Awarded for deliberate hand or arm contact.

Stand back ten yards
For the opposition team at a free kick.

Play on
The referee lets the play continue.

Indirect free kick
Given for obstruction.

Kicking foul
Player deliberately kicked.

Pushing foul
Player pushed off ball.

Foul throw-in
Feet over side-line.

Tripping foul
Player deliberately tripped.

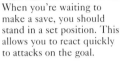

READY TO SAVE

The goalkeeper is one of the most important players in a team. If you think you've got what it takes to be one, then the first step is to learn the vital skills of quick movement around the goal area and reliable handling.

GOALKEEPER'S STANCE

When you're waiting to make a save, you should stand in a set position. This allows you to react quickly to attacks on the goal.

This is the typical stance used by goalkeepers. It shows you are alert and ready.

Try to lean forwards slightly so you are ready to make quick and sudden falls or jumps.

Your legs should be slightly bent, and about a shoulder width apart.

Your weight should be equally balanced on the balls of your feet.

Keep your head still and your eyes on the ball.

Your hands should be at around waist height with palms facing outwards.

WHAT TO WEAR

A cap or visor keeps the sun out of your eyes when dealing with high balls.

Wear loose, comfortable clothes. Diving and bending isn't easy in tight clothes.

A shirt with padded elbows and shoulders helps to protect you when you dive.

Gloves with latex palms help to give you much more grip on the ball.

On hard ground, wear tracksuit bottoms to protect your knees.

MOVING AROUND THE GOAL AREA

When you are comfortable with the keeper's stance, you can practise moving quickly around the goal area. If you can move well, catches are much easier to take, as you get more of your body behind the ball. Try moving in the set position, taking small sideways steps. Don't cross your feet as it can slow you down. Then ask a team-mate to move backwards and forwards across the penalty area. Try to mirror his movements.

Try to mirror your team-mate's movements.

Don't open your legs too wide.

THE W SHAPE

For shots or headers that come towards you at chest or head height, the most effective catching technique is the W shape. The palms of your hands face outwards and your index fingers and thumbs form a 'W' around the back of the ball. Your fingers need to be spread wide and thumbs should be about an inch or two (2-5cm) apart.

As the shot approaches, you need to keep your eyes on the ball. If you look away from the ball, this could mean a dropped catch and a rebound to an opponent.

Keep your hands well in front of your body, so you can watch the ball as you catch it.

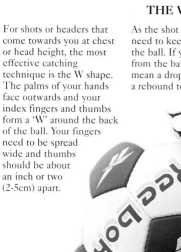

Make sure your fingers are relaxed and flexible so that they absorb the impact of a shot. The ball might bounce out of rigid, tense hands.

This is how your hands should look when you catch using the W shape.

CATCHING AND MOVING

This game will help you to practise combining your sideways movement in the set position with taking catches at chest or head height.

Lay out a zigzag pattern of sports markers on a pitch with a gap of about 2m (6ft) between each one. Weave through the markers, staying in the set stance.

After you catch, bring the ball close in to your body, so that it cannot slip out of your hands.

Ask a team-mate to throw or kick shots at chest or head height. He should vary the direction of the throws, aiming to your sides as well as straight ahead.

SHOTS NEAR THE KEEPER

Some shots come too quickly for you to have time to do a kneeling or bending save. When you need to get down to the ball as fast as possible, falling to the ground is the best solution. Practising falling saves will help you get ready to try diving saves later on.

THE COLLAPSING SAVE

When a ball is aimed close to you, there is no need to dive for it. What you should do instead is move quickly out of the set stance and collapse onto the shot. When you do a collapsing save, swing your legs to one side and drop down to the ball hands first. Your body will act as a barrier behind your hands. Try not to land on your elbows (see page 86).

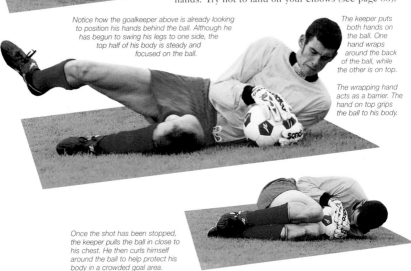

Notice how the goalkeeper above is already looking to position his hands behind the ball. Although he has begun to swing his legs to one side, the top half of his body is steady and focused on the ball.

The keeper puts both hands on the ball. One hand wraps around the back of the ball, while the other is on top.

The wrapping hand acts as a barrier. The hand on top grips the ball to his body.

Once the shot has been stopped, the keeper pulls the ball in close to his chest. He then curls himself around the ball to help protect his body in a crowded goal area.

COLLAPSING TIPS

★ You should practise collapsing saves regularly, because many keepers find them very difficult to do.

★ Don't overdo your collapsing movement. It shouldn't involve any jumping or acrobatic leaps.

★ The ball will be moving fast, so get your hands down in time, otherwise the ball will squeeze under your body.

This keeper didn't move fast enough.

SAVING WITH YOUR FEET

When a shot is fired in from very close range, you will need to react fast to make a save. If you don't have time to get your hands to the ball, you'll have to save with your feet and legs.

As the ball approaches, keep your weight well balanced and turn your feet outwards. Watch the ball very closely and try to use your legs as a barrier.

Saving with your feet should only be attempted as a final option. This type of save is instinctive and you have no control over where the ball rebounds to.

Saving with your feet is a good reflex reaction when a shot comes at you through a crowd of players.

PREPARING FOR DIVING SAVES

Diving saves involve a lot of falling on the ground. Here are two games to give you more practice in this, before you learn how to dive. It's best to practise with another keeper, who can also get used to falling.

1. Your team-mate rolls the ball through your legs. Turn around quickly and fall on the ball before it is out of your reach.

2. Your team-mate throws balls a metre (3ft) either side of you. Crouch down to catch them, falling on your side as you catch.

HANDS AND FEET PRACTICE

Mark out a goal about 4m (13ft) wide within the goal area. Place two more markers the same distance apart about 3m (10ft) out from goal. Do the same again about 6m (20ft) out.

Ask a team-mate to stand on a line level with either set of markers and take shots at goal. Swap with your team-mate when you feel tired. Use your hands to save whenever possible.

Practise collapsing saves for longer shots.

Save with your feet and legs for closer, faster shots.

DIVING SAVES

When attackers fire wider shots at goal, you'll need to attempt a diving save. Successful acrobatic diving saves give goalkeepers a lot of satisfaction and can make the difference between winning or losing a match. However, there is much more to a diving save than simply leaping into the air. The right jumping and landing techniques are essential.

A DIVING CATCH

When you spot the 'flight', or direction, of the ball, take a few quick sideways paces to reduce your diving distance. Stay focused on the ball in the set stance.

Just before you are about to dive, quickly transfer your weight onto the foot nearest the incoming ball. Push down hard on this foot and then begin to leap up.

Try to get as much thrust or 'spring' from your leg as possible. As you leap up, keep your eyes on the ball and dive slightly forwards to attack the shot.

Use the W shape catching technique, letting your hands absorb the power of the shot. Grasp the ball tightly so that it doesn't bounce out of your hands when you land.

A SAFE LANDING

It's vital to learn a safe landing technique. When you hit the ground, try to land on your side, as this is a well cushioned part of the body. Don't come down on your elbows or your stomach.

Keep your body relaxed as you land.

If you are playing on an artificial surface or on hard ground, tracksuit bottoms can help prevent painful grazes to the knees.

THE CAT

Many diving saves require impressive agility and suppleness.

In the 1960s and '70s, Peter Bonetti of Chelsea and England became known as 'The Cat', because of his quick reflexes and diving technique.

TIPPING THE BALL

You should aim to catch most diving saves, but if a shot is too powerful or too well-placed to catch, you should still try to get a touch on the ball as it goes by.

A slight deflection, or tip, of the ball can be enough to push it off target. When the shot touches your hand, make sure your palm is open and your fingers are spread wide. Try to push or flick the ball away.

Use only one hand to deflect the ball.

Keeping your palm open makes a bigger target for the ball to hit.

When you deflect the ball away, try to tip it over the bar or around the post.

PLAY SAFE

If you push the ball straight out in front, you could give it to an opposing striker.

The safest option is putting it out of play for a corner. You can tip the ball with either hand as you dive, but try to use the hand nearest the ball. Use your upper hand for tipping over the bar, and your lower hand for pushing the ball around the post.

DIVING TIPS

★ It is better to use swift footwork to get closer to the ball and make an easier save than to attempt a difficult diving save.

★ All keepers have a favourite diving side but you should be a strong diver on both sides. Spend extra time building up your weaker spring.

IMPROVING YOUR DIVES

This game helps you get used to the hard impact with the ground that follows a diving save. It can also strengthen your spring off the ground. Ask a team-mate or another keeper to shoot or throw the ball just inside either post of a full size goal. Stand in the middle of the goal before each shot and as the ball approaches, leap up off the foot nearest the ball. Swap around after four or five diving saves.

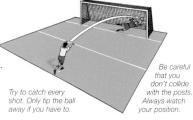

Try to catch every shot. Only tip the ball away if you have to.

Be careful that you don't collide with the posts. Always watch your position.

POSITIONING

In goalkeeping, good positional sense is as important as sound handling skills, especially when the ball is in the defending third of the pitch. Good positioning involves skilful footwork and getting your body behind the ball. This makes a lot of saves easier for you and also makes shooting at goal harder for your opponents.

GETTING IN LINE

Keepers like to position themselves somewhere on an imaginary line between the ball and the centre of the goal. This is known as being in line with play.

This keeper is in line with play and so as a shot comes in, he can get his body behind the ball and make a simple save.

Here the keeper hasn't managed to keep in line with play. As a shot approaches, he is at full stretch and has to make a much more difficult save.

NARROWING THE ANGLE

Good keepers not only need to be in line but off their goal-line too. By coming off the goal-line, keepers reduce the view of the goal for attackers and 'narrow' the shooting angle. Shots become much easier for the keeper to reach.

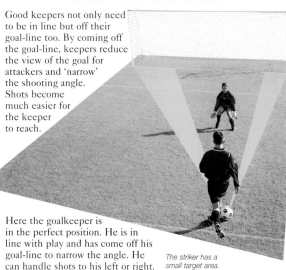

Here the goalkeeper is in the perfect position. He is in line with play and has come off his goal-line to narrow the angle. He can handle shots to his left or right.

The striker has a small target area.

Here the keeper is in trouble. He is out of position and has left both sides of the goal wide open. He hasn't narrowed the angle, so the striker can close in on goal (see also page 49).

This striker has a clear view of the goal and can easily aim a powerful shot either side of the keeper.

IN THE DEFENDING THIRD

You should always be in line when the ball is in your defending third of the pitch. How far off your goal-line you should be depends on where play is taking place, and if you think that your goal area is under threat of attack from a sudden shot or cross.

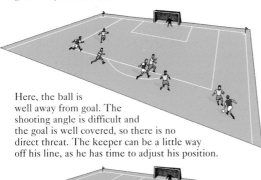

Here, the ball is well away from goal. The shooting angle is difficult and the goal is well covered, so there is no direct threat. The keeper can be a little way off his line, as he has time to adjust his position.

Here, the attack is inside the penalty area and the striker will soon be in a position to shoot. The keeper must not be too far off his goal-line as he is directly involved in play. He must be well in line with the ball.

THE CHIP SHOT

A keeper should be well off his line and in touch with play when the opposition are on the attack, but he mustn't rush out too fast.

This keeper is rushing out to narrow the angle.

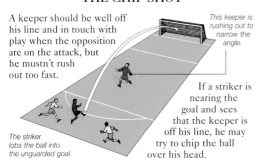

The striker lobs the ball into the unguarded goal.

If a striker is nearing the goal and sees that the keeper is off his line, he may try to chip the ball over his head.

RECOVERING POSITION

You must always be ready to change your position quickly. A sudden sideways pass near or inside the penalty area will leave you well out of line. You need to get in line again fast, before an attacker can shoot into the open space.

Here, player A passes to player B. The keeper should move from position 1, where he was covering player A, to position 2 to line up against player B. By making a direct diagonal movement, he will get into position sooner.

THE ANGLES GAME

This game helps you practise getting in line with play and narrowing shooting angles. Ask two team-mates, each with a ball, to stand on either side of the penalty area about 14m (46ft) out from goal.

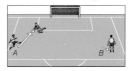

Get into line, shout 'ready' and then save from player A.

Do the same with player B. A and B should vary their positions before each shot.

HANDLING CROSSES

Many goals come from high crosses aimed deep into the penalty area. Every cross is different, and you need to decide whether to come for a cross or leave it for your defence to clear. Catch a cross if you can, but punch or tip if you have to. If you decide to deal with a cross, be positive and go for the ball.

POSITIONING FOR CROSSES

Where you stand for a cross depends on where the crosser is. Half turn your body towards the crosser so that you can watch movements in the area as well as the ball.

Here, the ball is near the wing and a long way out from goal. The keeper is positioned in the centre of the goal so that he won't be left stranded by a cross over his head. Moving backwards and catching a ball under pressure isn't easy.

This keeper is about 3m (10ft) off the goal-line, so he can easily reach a cross aimed 10-12m (33-39ft) from the goal.

Play has now moved away from the wing and well into the attacking third of the pitch. The keeper is moving closer to the near post to narrow the angle. He must still be alert to the chance of a far post cross.

This keeper is now about 1m (3ft) off his line as the cross is likely to be delivered low and hard into the goal area.

A CLEAN CATCH

You need good communication with your defence when dealing with a cross. If you decide you can definitely reach an incoming cross and can make a good, clean catch without other players getting in your way, then clearly shout 'Keeper's ball!' as you take a running jump for it.

Jump off one leg and catch the ball about 30cm (1ft) in front of your face, using the W shape.

Lift up the leg nearest to the opposition to protect your lower body against challenges.

As you jump, turn sideways on to the opposition and face the ball. Try to catch a cross when the ball is at its highest point. This makes it harder for strikers to get up and reach the ball. When you have dealt with a cross, be ready to make a quick throw (see page 92) to start an attack.

TWO-HANDED PUNCHES

Sometimes other players can get in your way or put you under so much pressure that you are unable to catch the ball. In this case, try to punch it away instead. A good punched clearance needs height and distance to give you enough time to recover your position if the ball goes straight to an opponent.

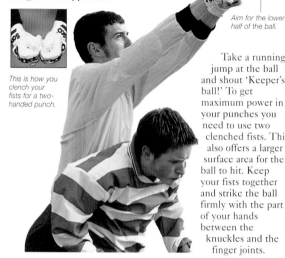

Aim for the lower half of the ball.

This is how you clench your fists for a two-handed punch.

Take a running jump at the ball and shout 'Keeper's ball!' To get maximum power in your punches you need to use two clenched fists. This also offers a larger surface area for the ball to hit. Keep your fists together and strike the ball firmly with the part of your hands between the knuckles and the finger joints.

ONE-HANDED PUNCHES

If you can't get two hands to the ball, you may have to use a less powerful one-handed punch.

One-handed punches are quite difficult to do because you only have a small punching surface.

When the ball is drifting over your head, and you have to move backwards quickly, a one-handed punch will strike the ball out of danger towards the opposite wing.

TIPPING

If an inswinging cross is aimed deep into the goal area and you are under a lot of pressure, you could try tipping the ball over the bar for a corner (see page 87).

Use the hand which is furthest from the goal, to get a much bigger swing at the ball.

When you tip the ball out for a corner, you are giving possession straight back to the opposition. A catch or strong punch is safer.

CROSSES GAME

This game should get you used to handling under pressure and timing your jumps. Stand in the centre of a goal and ask two team-mates, each with a ball, to supply crosses from the wings.

Ask your team-mates to vary the height and pace of the crosses.

This team-mate acts as an opposing striker, trying to beat you to the ball. Team-mates could swap roles regularly.

THROWING

Accurate and reliable distribution of the ball to your team-mates is an essential skill for a keeper. Well placed throws or kicks can lead to dangerous attacks on your opposition's goal. There are three main types of throw and each can be effective in opening up space for an unmarked team-mate.

THE UNDERARM ROLL

For an underarm throw, start by swinging your throwing arm back.

You use the underarm roll when you are aiming for a team-mate no more than 8m (26ft) away. As he will be positioned near the goal, use this throw when no opponents are close by. Don't use this type of throw on muddy pitches, as the ball might get stuck.

Get down quite low. Your front foot should point in the direction of the throw.

Swing your throwing arm forwards, releasing the ball at the last moment.

Keep the ball low, rolling it along the ground.

THE JAVELIN THROW

Use the javelin throw to cover distances of up to 15m (49ft). Your target might be a team-mate who has moved into space on the wing or who has dropped back from midfield. Javelin throws should be delivered low and fast to their target, so try not to throw the ball too high in the air.

Bend your knees slightly to help keep the ball low as you release it.

Bend your throwing arm back and bring the ball up level with your shoulder. Aim your non-throwing arm at the target and point your front foot in the same direction.

Swing your throwing arm forwards quickly and release the ball. Flicking your wrist will help keep the ball low. For extra distance on your throw, follow through powerfully.

THE OVERARM THROW

Use the overarm throw to cover distances of 15m (49ft) or more. When your technique is well developed, the overarm throw can travel nearly as far as a kick. This throw is very good for getting the ball upfield quickly once an opposition attack has broken down. A fast, well placed throw can leave opponents badly out of position and can turn defence into attack.

Bring your throwing arm back behind your body. Keep it straight. Point your non-throwing arm and your front foot at the target.

Swing your throwing arm powerfully upwards and over your shoulder.

Transfer your weight onto your front foot. To get height on the throw, release the ball when your arm is at its highest point.

WHEN TO THROW

★ Use a throw after cutting out a cross. You can change the direction of play while opponents are still in your defending third.

★ If the opposing team has a tall defence, low throws are a lot better than high kicks for keeping possession.

★ When you are playing in a strong wind, use throws rather than kicks, as they are easier to direct and control.

★ Stick to throwing if you are not a strong kicker. Good throws are better than weak kicks.

WHERE TO THROW

Most throws should be aimed towards the sides of the pitch, where a team-mate may be able to find some space to run into.

Aim for the safest part of the pitch.

A throw aimed into the crowded centre of the pitch will be difficult to control and could be easily intercepted. As most throws travel quite low through the air, you shouldn't try to throw over the heads of opponents.

THROWING GAME

Ask two keepers to help you with this game so you can all practise your throwing skills. Form a triangle, 6m (20ft) apart, and roll the ball underarm to each other first.

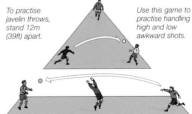

To practise javelin throws, stand 12m (39ft) apart.

Use this game to practise handling high and low awkward shots.

For overarm practice, two throwers stand about 15m (49ft) apart. The other keeper stands in the middle and tries to intercept the throws.

KICKING

Place kicks, volleys and half-volleys give you an opportunity to send the ball a long way upfield, changing defence into attack. Keepers need to be strong accurate kickers, so practise regularly.

THE PLACE KICK

A place kick is a kick taken when the ball is stationary, such as a goal kick or free kick. Long, powerful place kicks help ease pressure on your defence. If your kicks don't travel very far, make sure they are accurate.

Take an angled run-up and put your non-kicking foot to the side of the ball. Your kicking foot swings forwards quickly.

As you kick, lean back slightly and keep your eyes fixed on the ball.

Strike the lower half of the ball with your instep. Follow through powerfully.

THE VOLLEY

To do a volley, you drop the ball from your hands and kick it before it hits the ground. When you are holding the ball, you must release it within six seconds (see page 58). The higher you aim a volley, the longer it will take to reach its target.

As you run, hold the ball in front of you at waist height. Take a good backswing as the ball drops.

Place your non-kicking leg behind the ball. Leaning back slightly will help to get lift on the kick.

Keeping your head steady, kick the bottom of the ball with your instep. Follow-through smoothly.

THE HALF-VOLLEY

When you do a half-volley, the ball bounces once before you kick it. Use half-volleys in windy conditions, as they do not travel as high through the air as volleys. It's risky to try them on muddy or uneven pitches.

Drop the ball from about waist height. It should land just in front of your non-kicking foot.

As the ball bounces, swing your kicking leg forwards, leaning back as you kick.

Watching the ball carefully, strike the bottom half of it with your instep.

WHICH KICK TO CHOOSE

Think carefully about what type of kick to use and don't take any chances. Aim all place kicks to the sides of the pitch, and never kick across the penalty area. Only kick over your opponents' heads with high volleys or half-volleys.

If you are a strong kicker, you might be able to reach the attacking third with a powerful volley.

Half-volleys travel more quickly than volleys and so are good for starting fast, unexpected attacks.

Place kicks aimed to the sides of the pitch are safer and might find team-mates in space.

If your strikers are not good at heading the ball, a short kick to a defender is better than a kick upfield.

TARGET PRACTICE

You will need five or six balls for this game which will improve the accuracy and distance of your kicks. Ask another keeper to help you. Take turns at kicking and retrieving the balls.

For place kicks, kick alternately from either corner of the goal area, aiming inside two markers 6m (20ft) apart on the halfway line.

For volleys, position markers level with the circle in the other half of the pitch.

For place kicks, position the markers equally between the centre circle and the touchline.

For half-volleys and volleys, kick from the edge of the penalty area. Try to clear the markers in the opposition's half of the pitch.

INDEX

Answers to the offside quiz on page 79:

1) Offside (the offside player receives the ball indirectly from the throw-in) 2) Not offside (the offside player is not interfering with play) 3) Offside (he is in a position which gives him an advantage) 4) Not offside (he dribbles through).

With special thanks to soccer players Osman Afzal, Brooke Astle, Sajid Aziz, Kevin Better, Botlme Bolotete, Carl Brogden, Nathan Brooks, David Buckley, Nicola Burton, John Cox, Ben Dale, Leanne Davis, Deps Gabonamong, James Peter Greatrex, Gemma Grimshaw, Mohammed Gulfam, Alicia Hardiker, Rachel Horner, David Hughes, Moynul Islam, John Jackson, Lindsey Jamieson, Michael Jones, Sarah Leigh, Andrum Mahmood, Nathan Miles, Otlaadisa Mohambi, Andrew Perkin, Leanne Prince, Matthew Rea, Peter Riley, Daniel Savastano, Mohammad Usman Shafiq, Christopher Sharples, Ciaran Simpson, Jody Spence, John Tabas, Ben Tipton, Mark Travis, Joe Vain, Christopher White, Neil Wilson, David Wood, and to their coaches, Dave Benson, Alex Black, Bryn Cooper, Warren Gore and Gavin Rhodes.

Picture Acknowledgements: p25 DENIS LOVROVIC/AFP/Getty Images; p30 Jamie McDonald/Getty Images; p32 Rick Stewart/Getty Images; p34 THOMAS COEX/AFP/Getty Images; p40 Mike Hewitt/Getty Images; p50 Shaun Botterill/Getty Images; p53, p57 Matthew Peters/Manchester United via Getty Images; p61 TOSHIFUMI KITAMURA/AFP/Getty Images; p67 Paul Gilham/Getty Images; p80 Phil Cole/Getty Images; p86 STAFF/AFP/Getty Images.
Every effort has been made to trace the copyright holders of the material in this book. If any rights have been omitted, the publishers offer to rectify this in any subsequent editions following notification.